Love's Falling Star

by

B.D. Grayson

2021

LOVE'S FALLING STAR
© 2021 By B.D. Grayson. All Rights Reserved.

ISBN 13: 978-1-63555-873-9

This Trade Paperback Original Is Published By
Bold Strokes Books, Inc.
P.O. Box 249
Valley Falls, NY 12185

First Edition: March 2021

Credits
Editor: Cindy Cresap
Production Design: Stacia Seaman
Cover Design by Tammy Seidick

Acknowledgments

To Jaycie Morrison. Thank you for the time you put into helping me during this journey. There aren't enough words to express my gratitude for your friendship and guidance. I will forever be thankful we met.

To my wife, Tammy. Thank you for your encouragement and always believing in my dream. I will always remember reading to you about Lochlan and Vanessa as you cooked dinner each night. I feel like we did this one together, which makes it even more special. Just like everything else, I wouldn't be where I am without you.

Chapter One

Lochlan Paige strummed the guitar in her hands just as the spotlight moved from her to scan the sold-out stadium. Her racing heart was full at the roar of the crowd. These moments were what she lived for. The fame was nice, the money was good, but it was these moments that were a high. She had worked for years to get where she was in the country music business. Hearing these people, and the ground-shaking cheers, was like a reward for the blood, sweat, and tears she put into her dream.

The spotlight found her again. "Thank you all for coming out tonight, Raleigh. See y'all next year." Just before she took a bow, Lochlan wondered if there would ever be a feeling better than these moments. There would never be anything that would take the place of the excitement performing to a crowd this size. This was her life. Her world. Her only love.

When she straightened, she waved and smiled the smile that she knew had her sitting atop every beautiful person list in the entertainment business. Lochlan Paige was the hottest concert ticket in country music and was the second highest paid female artist in all of music, and she sold out stadiums in record time.

It had been nearly seven years since she first stepped on a stage, and tonight, she was saying good-bye to her loyal fans for a few months, as her concert season was ending. After five years of headlining tours, countless talk shows, and guest appearances, the end of the season was both a sad and a welcome break. It was hard to smile when you were exhausted, but she wasn't afforded the luxury of letting that stop her. She waved as she exited the stage, and immediately, there were hands on her. Stagehands removed her ear monitors and the battery pack from the back of her pants as they told her what an amazing job she had done.

She was followed into the dressing room by only one person, Jamie Holt. Jamie wore a multitude of hats for Lochlan. Jamie was her manager, personal assistant, best friend since childhood, and most importantly, therapist. Jamie had kept her most guarded secret since high school, that Lochlan was gay. And it was Jamie who bore the wrath of Lochlan's life of hiding on nights Lochlan was at her loneliest.

Jamie texted on her phone. "Okay, we have a handful of meet and greets still left."

"What? How was that not handled before the show?"

"These are different, Loc. It's some of the stadium staff."

"When you say staff, you mean…"

"God, Loc, cut me some slack here. I'm doing my best. They only wanted to meet with you briefly."

"Who are 'they'?" Lochlan made air quotes with her hands as she sighed.

"'They,'" Jamie returned the quotes, "are three guys from the football team."

"I hate doing stadiums. What happened to arenas and fairgrounds? I miss those, ya know? Hell, you never had a cow that demanded a meet and greet when I'm exhausted."

"Please warn me the moment cows start speaking to you. We need to seriously look at cutting dates back at that point. That is more therapy than any of my degrees prepared me for."

"I'm serious, Jamie. I'm tired." Lochlan hung her shoulders.

"It's just a few autographs…and maybe a picture or two." Jamie sighed.

"You mean it's just a few guys who want to smile at me, be polite, and think that I need a date to the next series of award shows. Well, you know what?"

"You don't need it," Jamie answered, rubbing her forehead in what Lochlan knew was frustration.

"You're damn right I don't need it. God! I just want to go home."

"And you will, Loc. Just give me half an hour. I swear. It's the last night before you have a couple of months off."

Jamie seemed tired too. She probably didn't want this any more than Lochlan did. Changing the subject, she asked, "Did you find me one?"

"A library?"

"Mm-hmm," Lochlan said as she began to walk into the bathroom.

"Like I said, this is it. We're done for the season and I didn't think you needed one." As Lochlan turned the shower on, she heard Jamie again. "You were just complaining about needing to go home and rest. By the way, are you staying in Knoxville or heading back home to Nashville? I need an answer, Loc. They're getting low on seats."

"I do need to rest," Lochlan yelled from the other room. "But I have this song stuck in my head. I'd like to get it on paper, and I'm probably going to Knoxville. It's been a while since I've seen Mom and Dad."

After a moment, Jamie said, "Okay, it looks like there's a twenty-four-hour library about five miles from here. It's sitting just off a college campus, and considering it's Saturday night, I doubt anyone is there."

Lochlan yelled over the shower again. "Great. Just me and the dateless bookworms who probably have no idea who Lochlan Paige is. Just the way that I like it."

"Don't be ridiculous, even the dateless bookworms know who you are."

Lochlan emerged from the shower and removed the shower cap on her head. She threw a snug-fitting long-sleeved black shirt over her head and began putting her jeans on. "So, we'll meet with these guys and go, right?"

"Yes." Jamie handed Lochlan her shoes. "I wish you had told me that you wanted to write. I could have arranged to have a private area of the library like usual."

"I didn't know until just before showtime. It just hit me, and I want to get this written down."

"All right, I'll get Jacob to head over with you."

"I don't need my bodyguard."

"It will be after midnight, you aren't going alone, and as much as I love you, I have a plane back to Knoxville to catch."

Lochlan smiled. "Wow, aren't we in a hurry to get home?"

"I haven't seen my husband in three weeks and have probably forgotten the color of my own toothbrush." Jamie frowned. "That, however, isn't an admission of guilt. It's just a possibility."

"It's not the orange one. God knows that one belongs to Eli."

"The man doesn't know they make another color besides Tennessee orange, and that's part of the reason I love him. And yes, I'm in a hurry to get home."

"Okay. We'll hurry and get you home to that sexy husband of yours."

"Thank you. And you *will* take Jacob with you."

"Yes, ma'am."

One hour later, she was walking into the library in a

baseball cap pulled down low and her ponytail pulled out the back. There were only a handful of people in the building, and if anyone recognized Lochlan, they didn't show it. Maybe they just respected the effort she had taken not to be recognized, or maybe it was the six-foot-five, two-hundred-fifty-pound man who walked close behind her. She wasn't sure but was grateful either way.

She went up the staircase to the second level of the extraordinarily sized open room, while Jacob stayed on the bottom level to give her privacy. He made sure that he could clearly see her from where he sat. As she found a spot between two rows of books, Lochlan pulled out her tablet and opened the keyboard app, snugly tucked her earbuds in, and clicked her pen open. She knew Jamie didn't understand, but *this* was home. To Lochlan, home was in the form of her pen, paper, and iPad app. People say that home is where you're loved and safe. Writing sometimes seemed to be the only place that felt like home. She did prefer her baby grand piano, but this was the next best thing.

She started jotting lyrics on the paper and tapping the keyboard. It didn't matter that it was small; it made music, and that was all Lochlan needed it to do. She was lost in the melody that was playing inside her head until there was a tap on her shoulder. She looked up fully expecting to see Jacob, but the woman who stood above her was not her oversized protector. It wasn't just a woman, this one was gorgeous with dark hair and the most amazing brown eyes that Lochlan had ever seen.

Lochlan quickly removed the earbuds. "Hi." She smiled.

"You do realize that you're supposed to be quiet in here, right?"

"Um, yeah. I mean, I know the rules." Lochlan stumbled over her reply. "Sorry, I didn't realize I was being loud."

"The humming is distracting."

"Sorry, I didn't realize that was happening."

The woman seemed to soften as she dropped her crossed arms to her sides. "Just try and be a little quieter. I've read the same line three times listening to you."

Lochlan smiled. "Well, at least tell me that it was good."

"It wasn't horrible."

"Please tell me that your definition of not horrible means at least remotely decent."

"I have a paper due on Monday, so I would say anything in this library that isn't the anatomy of the human body is remotely decent."

"I'll take that. I'm really sorry, and I'll try to be quiet."

"Thanks, and I'll let you get back to your…" she gestured to the pen and tablet in Loc's hands, "music."

"My bosses will thank you."

"Bosses? You write music?" she asked as she raised one of her perfectly formed eyebrows.

Lochlan chuckled. It never entered her mind that someone would truly have no idea who she was. "Yeah, I do."

"Oh wow. Do you mean for commercials and things?"

Lochlan laughed. "Ouch. No, I don't do commercials. I mean, I have done commercials, but not the jingles for them, no."

"Oh, well, okay. I have a paper that, against all my wishes, isn't writing itself."

Lochlan smiled. "Good luck with the paper, and again, sorry to bother you."

"Well, good luck with the music."

Lochlan watched her walk away. Damn, if that was what nerdy, dateless bookworms looked like, she'd take two. She shook her head and placed the earbuds back in her ears. This time she remained quiet for the next two hours.

When she was done, Lochlan stood and dusted off her jeans, placing all her items in her bag. As she was emerging from the aisle, she saw the table where the woman was seated, still concentrating on the books in front of her as she made notes on a small laptop. Lochlan couldn't seem to help herself as she made her way toward the table.

As she approached, the woman looked up just in time to give Lochlan a deadly smile. "Music done?"

"It is. For now, anyway."

The woman lowered her dark-rimmed glasses. Lochlan thought she had seen many attractive people, but there was something about this one that made everything she did seem... sexy. *Who knew I had a thing for smart chicks?*

"That's good."

"What?" Lochlan said, feeling a touch of panic. Had the bookworm just read her mind?

A chuckle softened the woman's face. "That you're done. That's good, I assume?"

That look of intrigue was making her nervous. Were they flirting, or was this connection between them just her imagination? Lochlan wondered if she was showing her cards to someone she didn't even know, but was spared making any decisions when a hand stretched out to her. "I'm Vanessa."

"Hi." Lochlan's mind sifted through the million aliases she'd used as they shook. "I'm..." *Damn it, speak!*

Vanessa burst out with laughter. "I know who you are. I may be in a library on a Saturday night, but I don't live under a rock."

"You asked me if I did commercials."

Vanessa laughed. "You are in jeans and a Tennessee Smokies cap."

Sweet Lord, she's a baseball fan. "You like baseball?" Lochlan asked.

"What? You look surprised. Yes, I like baseball. I thought you didn't want me to know who you were. Plus, I get to tell my best friend, Mia, that I met her favorite singer and current celebrity girl crush. Getting to admit that I jerked her around a little will only make the story better. It'll be a story we're talking about for years to come."

Lochlan feigned shock. "That is just hateful."

"Hateful? This coming from someone who thought I was so—what, nerdy—that I didn't know who"—she leaned forward—"Lochlan Paige was. Now *that* is hateful, Ms. Paige."

Lochlan knew perfectly well Vanessa was playing her, yet she was falling right into her hands. She couldn't seem to stop continuing to be roped in. "I mean—I just thought—" *Why can't I fucking speak?* She took a deep breath. "I always feel like the real me in these places. I'm not Lochlan Paige here. It's just me. Loc."

"You should let people see you more."

"Lots of people see me. Hell, an entire stadium just saw me."

"Not this way. I like this you, and I barely know you." Vanessa stood and loaded her books into her leather briefcase satchel. "You know what else I like?" Lochlan shook her head. "Coffee."

"Me too."

"There's a café around the corner that's usually empty this time of night. Maybe no one would recognize you there. Wanna grab a coffee?"

"Coffee at three in the morning? Now that's hardcore."

"I'm a med student. I haven't seen my bed in four years." Lochlan raised her eyebrow, which Vanessa chose to ignore. "So, coffee?"

"Um, yeah. Let me just tell Jacob." Vanessa saw Jacob, who was watching them intently.

"Oh. I didn't realize you were with someone."

"He's the lucky bodyguard who my manager forced to come with me. Trust me, Jacob will stay out of the way. He just needs to know what I'm doing."

"Okay. It's just down the street on the right. I'll meet you there?"

"Yeah." Lochlan smiled at Vanessa. "I'll see you there."

Lochlan wondered what in the hell was she doing. This could be a total disaster. She didn't know Vanessa. She could do anything. Sell a story to the tabloids or call her friends and tell them where she was. There were a million ways this could go sideways, but for reasons unknown to Lochlan, she trusted Vanessa.

Ignoring the fact that this could also be the first step in everything going horribly wrong, Lochlan let Jacob drive her to the café. When she stepped out of the car, her worst fear hit her in the face. The small café was packed. Had Vanessa led her into a trap?

CHAPTER TWO

H ey." Vanessa stepped out of the building. "Shit, I'm sorry. I forgot that we had a huge concert in town tonight. People are everywhere."

Vanessa seemed to be trying to shield her from anyone seeing her. "It's okay. Hell, I should have known." She smiled. "I was actually at said concert."

"You were?" Vanessa said playfully.

"I was. Had great seats. Next time maybe I can get you tickets. I don't want to brag, but I know people."

"That would be nice." Vanessa looked back toward the building. "I can order us a cup to go. There's a park across the street that's very well lit, and we can just—" Vanessa stopped. "God, that's a stupid idea with someone as well-known as you."

Lochlan took her by the arm. "Jacob, give me a second." Lochlan led them back toward her car. "It's a nice gesture, but maybe I should just go."

"I understand."

"I know we have Jacob here, but I'm not sure that us walking around in the middle of the night is a good idea." Lochlan was saying all the things she needed to say. She didn't want to leave. "I really would have liked to stay. I don't feel comfortable around a lot of people, but you've done nothing but make me feel at ease, and that isn't an easy task, even for people who know me well."

"I just know that if I were in your position I would want some normalcy to my life."

"There are very few things about my life that will ever be normal again." She chuckled and extended her hand. "It was a pleasure meeting you, Vanessa."

Vanessa took the hand. "You too." They looked at each other, still hand in hand. "Oh my God." Vanessa started digging through her bag. "I have got to at least have a picture with you—for my best friend, Mia."

"I can take the picture," she said, taking her phone out and adjusting it in front of them. They came cheek to cheek and smiled. "There. By morning your friend will see it, I assure you."

Vanessa smiled. "Should that scare me?"

"Maybe I'm the one that should be scared."

"I'm harmless, I promise," Vanessa said sincerely.

Lochlan stared at her for another moment too long before she took in a breath. "I should go."

"Okay. It was nice meeting you."

"You too." Lochlan smiled and stepped into the vehicle as Jacob closed the door behind her. As they drove away from Vanessa, she waved once more. Lochlan wondered in that moment what it would be like to be able to act on a connection with another woman. For all she knew Vanessa wasn't even gay. It was ridiculous to hope that she was. She looked at the picture of them and wondered if she could ever stop this charade of a life that she lived.

❖

Vanessa was sound asleep when someone began pounding at her bedroom door. *Nothing like being awakened by the heart-stopping fear of impending death by robber. Wait, robbers don't knock before entering.*

"What the hell?" Vanessa groaned as she threw the blanket back and sat up. "Come in!"

Vanessa was still rubbing her eyes when Mia opened the door with her second-best friend, Ty, in tow. "Where in the hell have you been?"

Vanessa looked at the clock on her desk. "It's nine thirty in the morning. I'm pre-med with a huge paper due on Monday. I was up half the night studying. Where do you think I've been? I've been in bed."

"Bed my ass! Explain this!" Mia held out her phone.

"What?" Vanessa took the device and reached over to the nightstand for her glasses. She slid them on, and her heart stopped when she saw what had caused the commotion. It was a picture posted to Lochlan Paige's Twitter account.

"It's posted to Instagram as well. Just in case you were wondering," Ty said.

The picture was of her and Lochlan, cheek to cheek with the caption, *Told you they would know by morning. Thanks for trying to help me stay hidden. It was nice meeting you and tell Mia I said hi.—Loc.*

"You actually met her last night?" Ty shouted. "And we, your best friends, hear about it on Twitter?" Vanessa smiled. "And where the hell is my 'hi' from Lochlan Paige?"

"Ty, you are a gay man who hates country music. I didn't realize that you would need one." Vanessa handed the phone back to Mia and climbed out of bed.

"We've been calling you for hours," Mia said.

"I'm sorry. It was four when I got in and I guess I just crashed."

Mia gasped. "You were with Lochlan Paige until four a.m.?"

"No, Mia. I just bumped into her last night." She made her way to the common area of the apartment.

Mia and Ty were on her heels. "I got three phone calls this morning from people asking where you were and if I had talked to you," Mia said.

"Well, now you have." Vanessa picked up the coffee pot. "And apparently, I'm up."

"I'm gonna need for you to go on both Instagram and Twitter and address this."

"This? There is no *this*," she said, looking through the cabinet. "Where did you hide my coffee?"

"Only you would be worried about coffee right now," Mia said.

"I was in the library last night and she was there, apparently writing a song or something."

Ty spoke up. "What was she like?"

"Nice. Sweet." Vanessa smiled. "She is so much prettier in person."

"Okay, now you're just rubbing it in." Mia groaned.

Vanessa chuckled. "Sorry. She wanted to be left alone last night, so I tried to do that. I didn't call you because I know that you would have brought fifteen other people."

"I would not—" Mia began, but Vanessa looked at her skeptically as she tilted her head in disbelief. "Okay, maybe I would have, but just a couple."

"She didn't want a couple."

"I'm gonna need for you to be a little less protective of her and worry about your best friend's needs a little more."

Vanessa hugged her. "Awwww. I love you, but this time I selfishly thought of me. I had Lochlan Paige all to myself."

"Oh my God, I knew it!" Mia gasped. "You were hogging the hot celebrity hoping to have a steamy tryst with her."

"A tryst? My God, you are reaching here. That only happens in movies and romance novels. Besides, Loc is straight."

"Loc? Did you just refer to Lochlan Paige as 'Loc,' the name that only other celebs and her friends call her?"

Vanessa laughed. "She told me to call her Loc. It just came out."

Mia walked quickly, and overdramatically, to the computer and turned it on. "Tweet her back!"

"Why?"

"Lochlan Paige has told you to call her by a name that is reserved for only certain people."

"And?" Vanessa asked as she returned to searching the cabinet. "Aha, there's the coffee."

"What really happened last night?" Ty asked.

"I told you. We were both there and she was humming all loud and I asked her to please be quiet."

"You what?" they both screamed in unison.

"I was trying to study."

"So, you told Lochlan Paige to what? Hush?" Ty laughed in shock.

Vanessa laughed at the horrified looks on their faces. "No. The word *hush* was never used."

"So, you politely told her to shut the hell up?" Ty glared at Mia. "This is your fault."

"My fault?" Mia gasped.

"Yes. She's a lesbian, so her interaction with other women is solely on you. My job is to call you a bitch when she needs me to and help her decorate this dungeon of a room."

Mia whipped her head to Vanessa. "You call me a bitch?"

"No!" Vanessa defended herself. "I have never, damn it, Ty."

"What?" he said defensively.

"And my room is not a dungeon."

"It is very plain, Nessa." Mia scanned the room.

Vanessa huffed loudly. "Okay." She went to the computer and sat down. She pulled up the account and then Lochlan's page. She couldn't help smiling at the picture. It was a really good photo of both of them.

Ty smiled. "I have to say, you two look—"

"Amazing together." Mia finished his thought in a dreamy voice.

"Yeah," he replied. "That."

Vanessa clicked on the picture and typed a reply.

Love the pic and meeting you, too. Mia says hi back. Also, my other BFF, Ty, feels left out and also says hello.

She clicked on the follow button and turned away from the computer. "There. Happy? She will probably never see it in the sea of tweets—" She stopped at the "ding" noise from the computer.

"Sweet Lord. Is that…?" Ty said as he and Mia rushed back to the computer.

"It's her!" Mia said giddily.

"It's her, what?" Vanessa asked. Then there was another beep.

"She followed you, faved the tweet, and retweeted it."

"Okay, the coffee is ready. Anyone want some?" Vanessa felt the increase of her heart rate with the unexpected turn her night had taken but refused to let anyone know.

"Forget about the damned coffee!" Ty said.

"Why? She just liked the post. It's not like she's trying to have a convers—"

The computer dinged again.

"You have a direct message." Mia said.

"Oh my God, they're falling in love before our very eyes. Hashtag blessed," Ty said.

"Good Lord, you're acting like children. No one is falling in love." She clicked on the direct message symbol.

Wallace, huh? I was kicking myself for not getting a last name. Does Mia like the pic? I think it's good. Oh, and tell Ty hello.

"This is not happening. Is this really happening to us right now?" Ty said as he fanned himself. "One day when she writes her tell-all memoir, we—Mia, you, and I—will be part of it."

Vanessa laughed at him as she typed back.

You're going to make Ty have some sort of breakdown at any moment. Yes, they liked the picture. Why wouldn't they? It's a great photo.

The computer sounded again.

Good. I'm just about to board the plane home. Glad you all like it. Good luck with the paper.

Vanessa didn't pay attention to the chaos and hyena volume of screeching that was going on behind her. She wondered, as she had last night, if a seemingly straight and very famous celebrity was flirting with her.

Thanks, and good luck on the song.

Thank you. Turning phone off. Airline bitches. LOL
Talk to you soon—I hope. Bye, Mia & Ty.

That was the last time the computer sounded. "What happened last night?" Ty asked.

"I-I'm not really sure, and now I'm even less sure. Is she—is she flirting with me? Isn't she straight?"

"Honey, it's country music. They're all straight until they aren't."

❖

Lochlan saw two familiar smiles as she and Jacob headed to baggage claim. "What are you doing here?" she said as she hugged Jamie's husband, Eli.

"Jamie didn't want you hailing a taxi or using Uber. So here we are." He saw Jacob and the guys exchanged hellos. "We got her from here."

"All right," Jacob said as he tugged Lochlan's baggage off the belt, along with his. "I'll just leave you all to it, then." He hugged Lochlan. "Let me know when you need me."

"Always do." She returned his hug, then waved as he left. She turned around to almost bump into Jamie. "What?"

"Who's the girl?" Jamie furrowed her brows.

"What girl?"

"Twitter girl. Instagram girl. Your notifications are exploding girl."

"She is a dateless, bookworm nerd that I met at the library."

"That beautiful woman is not a nerd. If she is, thank God nerds didn't look like that when we were in school. Us mediocre people would have been totally screwed."

Lochlan laughed. "She was hot, right?"

"Yes," Eli and Jamie answered in unison.

Lochlan smiled. "She was!" She looked more at Eli. "Did you see those eyes?"

"I did. Those things were—"

"Loc—" Jamie interrupted him.

"Let's just stop there. I already know what you're going to say next," Lochlan said.

"I'm sure that you do. That you cannot start acting on feelings that you have for women."

"I can't live in this bubble for the rest of my life. Hell, I'm nearly twenty-six years old and have had virtually no real relationships." Everything in Lochlan knew that Jamie was right, but no matter who was right or wrong, the reality of the situation had her upset.

"Loc, you met this girl last night in a library. This isn't something to derail your entire career over."

"This isn't about Vanessa."

"Oh, that's her name? Good to know, because somehow I think that I'm gonna be familiar with it."

"What's the deal?" Lochlan asked as she headed for the passenger seat of the car.

"The deal is that you are still very much a closeted star. If you are going to make a move, I need to know."

"I just met her last night, so don't marry us off yet."

"You've met a lot of people who didn't end up plastered all over the internet."

"She isn't fucking plastered, Jamie. It was one damn picture."

"One picture that has been retweeted fourteen thousand times in twelve hours."

"It was innocent!" Lochlan got into the car and slammed the door, leaving Jamie and Eli still standing outside.

CHAPTER THREE

Vanessa was sitting in her classroom and could feel every eye in the room on her. Her lab partner spoke without even looking at her. "Ignore them."

"That seems easier said than done." Vanessa sighed. "Three people that I don't even know came up to me today and asked me if Lochlan and I were friends. I would have thought the 'it's nice to meet you' tweet would have answered that question."

The girl next to Vanessa turned to her. "My freshman year, I dated the star running back. While we were dating, he was drafted to the NFL by the Raiders. People asked me every day if we were still dating. I understand this is vastly different, but my point is that tomorrow someone else will do something and you will be forgotten. Trust me, I was."

Lochlan noticed the hurt in her eyes. "Even by him?"

The girl smiled. "He tried not to, but it's a different world. They're in demand and there is always someone coming along who wants a piece of them…literally. He was a rookie in the NFL and people were throwing themselves at him. I can't imagine Lochlan Paige. God."

"Like I said, I don't even know her. We just met after the concert, I asked for a picture, and she took one. It's really all there is to it."

"Celebrities have a different life. Everyone that's seen with them is the new target. Thank God you aren't a man, or they would have you two married next week." She laughed.

Vanessa returned the laugh and hid an unsettling sadness. "Yeah, thank God."

❖

December in Nashville had turned cold as Lochlan sat in her living room. It had been a busy twenty-four hours. Yesterday, after the Grammy Awards announcement, her phone had rung constantly. There was the initial call from Jamie, then the record label, followed by producers, fellow artists and some of the Knoxville radio stations. Generally, she stayed off social media, as Jamie handled those type of things and would alert her of any social media that might need her attention, but she always liked to go back and check what her fans had written for herself.

As she sat, still in her warm pajamas, drinking coffee and listening to her fireplace crackle, she tucked her legs under her and pulled up her Twitter account. She wasn't sure how long she had been looking when she saw it.

@Vanessa_Wallace: Congrats on the Grammy nominations. Love the song and so does everyone else. #Winner #SongOfTheYear #AlbumOfTheYear #FemaleVocalistOfTheYear #RecordOfTheYear

Lochlan stared at the tweet for a while. It had been a few months since the night they met. Where Vanessa was concerned, her Twitter account had been completely silent since that night. Lochlan thought how busy Vanessa must be with school. "Probably doesn't have time for stuff like this."

Lochlan couldn't help but smile at the thought that Vanessa had gone out of her way to congratulate her. The thought wasn't lost on her that Jamie hadn't mentioned the tweet.

She clicked the direct message button and typed a reply.

Thanks for the tweet. Yesterday was crazy after the nominations were announced. Hope school is going well. I know you have a lot of tests coming up to end the semester, so good luck.

Lochlan went back to the tweets, liking Vanessa's, then continued reading the congratulations. An hour later, before closing her phone, she clicked on her gallery and looked at the picture that popped up. It was her and Vanessa. She smiled and took a sip of her coffee. It was a great picture and one that should have been a little less than flattering seeing as it was after three a.m. However, it wasn't. Lochlan couldn't help but think just how cute they were together. They stood almost even, resulting in a perfect cheek to cheek photo. Lochlan's blond hair was complemented by Vanessa's dark brown, and her dark eyes were a complete contrast to Lochlan's blue. Vanessa was effortlessly beautiful.

Lochlan closed the gallery knowing it was crazy to sit here and admire what looked like a gorgeous couple, when in fact it was two people who didn't even know each other. She could be a crazy serial killer for all Loc knew. She took a deep breath. "Please don't be a crazy serial killer."

❖

Vanessa sat in the library studying for her first exam of the semester. It was mid-January and she had met up with Mia and Ty yesterday as they gathered around the television to watch the Grammy Awards together. They cheered loudly as Lochlan won every award she'd been nominated for. There were pictures of her this morning on every news outlet and search engine. Vanessa loved the pictures of Lochlan with her arms full of Grammy trophies. They hadn't talked much since the nominations, just quickly exchanged holiday pleasantries. Each sent a merry Christmas and a happy New Year, and Vanessa added wishes of good luck as Lochlan performed in New York City for New Year's Eve. Other than those times, she hadn't heard from her. She had now accepted that there truly had been nothing that night. Lochlan was a singer who met someone and, as a good PR move, was very nice to them. She had heard of stuff like that before—stars meeting a fan and making them feel special. That was all this was, and she had finally accepted it.

Suddenly, there was someone next to her, and she looked over to see Mia. "What are you doing this weekend?" Mia asked.

Vanessa chuckled. "Same thing I do every weekend—study."

"Not this weekend you aren't. You and I are taking a road trip."

"A road trip? Where? Why would we need to be on a road trip?"

"Because my brother works for the Great Smokey Mountains Wildlife Preserve, and due to the damage done by the forest fires, they're having a fundraising concert and gala. He landed us two tickets and you are going."

"I really need to study—"

"One of the artists who's performing is a local talent by the name of Lochlan Paige. Heard of her?"

"What?" Mia now had Vanessa's attention.

"Lochlan had a concert scheduled this weekend in St. Louis. The stadium she was playing suffered some damage during the recent snowstorms, so she was suddenly available to do the fundraiser. When they added her this morning, my brother called and asked if I wanted tickets, soooo—"

Vanessa had to admit she really would like to see Loc again, but she didn't want to bother Lochlan, who was obviously just trying to be nice. "I really need to study this weekend."

"Too bad. He already has our tickets to the concert and the gala. We're leaving Friday after your morning class. It's a five-hour drive, so you'll have plenty of time to study on the way."

"The gala? That means—"

"That means we need clothes. Clothes that will turn the head of a very closeted superstar."

"Don't be ridiculous, Mia. Lochlan's head isn't turning for me. It was a one-time thing. Just let it go and tell Greg thank you for the tickets, but I can't go." She went back to her work. "Take Ty if you want someone to be there with you, but I'll pass."

"The tickets are *ours*, and you are going. Now, here's the deal, you either find something to wear, or when I kidnap you and throw you in the car, you will see Lochlan Paige again wearing jeans and a T-shirt."

"This is crazy. Why are we rushing to see someone who will barely remember me by now?"

"That's not the case and you should know it. Look, let's just go, and if she acts that way, we can leave. But we are going to try."

Vanessa sighed. "This is a bad idea."

"No, this is a fantastic idea."

❖

Lochlan entered the gala and was greeted by a swarm of fans. She was grateful for everyone who attended, but there was something about this part of these events that made her uneasy. She was used to being the center of attention, but when people crowded her, it was hard to hide the panic inside.

She looked out over the group of fans and her eyes wandered to a high-top table in the back of the room where Vanessa stood. Lochlan's knees almost went weak. *My God, she's beautiful.* The low-cut black dress and the way her hair fell to one side almost made Lochlan's mouth go dry. She smiled, incredibly pleased when Vanessa smiled back. Once she had greeted everyone who surrounded her, she made her way to Vanessa.

"You look—wow." Lochlan wasn't confident that she hadn't just undressed Vanessa with her eyes. And at the raise of Vanessa's eyebrow, she conceded she hadn't hidden it well.

A blush crept across Vanessa's face. "Thank you. You look amazing as well."

"How's school?"

"Good. Took a night off tonight." Vanessa turned to Mia. "Lochlan, this is my best friend, Mia."

Lochlan extended her hand. "It's so nice to meet you."

"Thank you. I'm a huge fan," Mia gushed.

"So I've heard." Lochlan smiled. She looked around. "And where is this Ty I've also heard about?"

"He has a family gathering tomorrow, so it's just a girls' weekend," Vanessa said.

"Then I'm glad you chose to spend it with us. It's a good cause, and as a hometown girl, it's something that I hold dear, so I'm thankful for everyone who came out to support it."

"Mia's brother works for the wildlife reserve, so he was able to get us tickets."

"It's nice to see a friendly face."

"I can imagine." Vanessa looked around the room. "It's a good crowd."

"It is, yes." Lochlan turned her attention to Mia. "Were you two able to see the show?"

"We were. You did amazing."

"Acoustic sets are always fun. You get to actually make eye contact with people and have a connection with them, versus large venues where there are so many faces and you try to give them all a moment of attention."

"Well, you did great." Vanessa beamed.

"Do you attend many concerts?" Lochlan asked.

Mia quickly responded. "If it's Brinley, you can count this one in." She pointed toward Vanessa.

"Oh, a Brinley fan?" Lochlan smiled as Vanessa looked away shyly, not answering at first. Her interest was also piqued at the mention of the pop singer, who was an out lesbian.

"We're a fan of the lesbians," Mia blurted out. Which caused Vanessa and Lochlan to both stare at her. "Not that you need to know any of that."

Lochlan wasn't sure how she should respond to the statement. "Well—that's—great."

Vanessa took a breath. "In high school, I was a proud member of her fan club, yes." She formed her hand to make the known fandom sign.

"Just in high school?" Lochlan loved the blush that came to Vanessa's face.

"Okay, maybe now too, but my taste in music does include country as well."

"Glad to hear that. Although she is a great person, and I'm happy for her success, it's nice to know that I have a chance to sway you toward country music."

Mia motioned to someone behind Lochlan. "I think someone is trying to get your attention."

Lochlan looked to see who it was. "Oh, that's Jamie, my best friend and manager." She couldn't ignore Jamie motioning urgently to join her. "Unfortunately, that's my cue." She smiled at Mia. "It was so nice meeting you." Then she caught Vanessa's gaze. "And as always, it was good seeing you."

"You, too."

"I'm really glad that you came. Maybe I can catch you again before the night is done."

"You're busy, Loc. We understand."

"Thank you for understanding. However, I will do my best to get back around to you." She placed the slightest of touches on Vanessa's arm. "Otherwise, I hope you enjoy your evening."

As they watched Lochlan walk away, Mia said, "She probably won't even remember me." She chuckled. "Yeah, right."

They spent the evening meeting several new people who worked with Mia's brother. Although they hadn't been able to talk to Lochlan any more that night, Vanessa had to admit that she had fun. She had glanced over at Lochlan a handful of times during the night and within moments always found blue eyes turning to her as well. The idea that Lochlan Paige seemed to be keeping up with her during the night had something in the pit of stomach doing cartwheels and accelerated her heart rate.

As the evening was winding down, Vanessa and Mia made their way from the ballroom to retrieve their coats. Vanessa hadn't wanted to bother Lochlan, thinking she would just direct message her later. As they were just about to leave the building, there was a hand on her shoulder. She turned to see a large man who apparently had been running to catch her. Vanessa had seen him before. She smiled. "Hi. Jacob, right?"

"Hi. Ms. Paige would like a word with you before you go."

Vanessa beamed as she saw Lochlan closing in on them. "Sorry, you were busy and we—"

"Were leaving without saying good-bye?" Lochlan dramatically placed a hand to her heart and feigned hurt, while the smile on her face never wavered.

"You've been otherwise occupied," Vanessa countered.

"I just wanted to tell you good night." She turned to Jacob. "Thanks, I have it from here." He nodded and returned inside. She turned back to them. "Thanks again for coming tonight. It was good seeing you, although I wish we'd had more time."

"Maybe next time," Vanessa said.

"I am so on board with there being a next time." Lochlan smiled.

Mia spoke up. "I'm going out to get in the valet line." She smiled at Lochlan again. "It was sooo nice meeting you."

"You as well." Once Mia was gone, she turned to Vanessa. "You know, the first time that I met you, you shielded me from people seeing me. You made me feel safe—protected. Tonight, you stood across the room quietly while I talked to everyone else and were very gracious about it. Not many fans do that."

"Not many megastars run me down before I leave the building."

Lochlan blushed. "Touché."

"So, I guess we're both seeing a different side to things tonight."

"Seems that way, yes."

"Is that what I am? Just a fan?" Vanessa asked.

"I hope not."

"Then just out of curiosity, why did you have your

bodyguard chase me down?" Lochlan stared nervously at the ground. "Why are you standing here now?"

After a few long seconds, Lochlan answered. "Can I get back to you on that?"

"You can. Just wanted to make sure that I'm seeing this right."

"Seeing what right?"

"That you seemed to be flirting with me." Vanessa held her breath awaiting a response.

"That would be crazy." Lochlan looked away, took a deep breath, and spoke more softly. "I am a country music singer whose career would be put in jeopardy if I were to do something like that...with someone I don't even know."

Vanessa understood exactly what that meant. "Right." Vanessa breathed deeply. "So, I guess that's settled." She tried to smile.

"Yeah, I guess so."

"No flirting happening here." Vanessa couldn't tell if Lochlan seemed more frustrated or just sad. "Good night, Lochlan."

A moment passed before Lochlan spoke. "Good night, Vanessa." They exchanged glances and Vanessa turned to go. She stopped when she heard Lochlan's quiet voice. "It would be crazy to think that someone would keep something like that a secret, right?" Vanessa turned and saw Lochlan's hand covering her mouth as if she was as shocked that she had spoken aloud as Vanessa was upon hearing it.

"What?" When Lochlan didn't answer, Vanessa moved toward her. "You know, you may meet someone one day that you can trust. Someone who just wanted to get to know you. No secrets to tell, no careers to jeopardize. Just someone who, for some reason, seems to be genuinely drawn to you."

Vanessa waited a beat before she finished. "If even to their own surprise."

"I would love to meet someone like that. Someone I could get to know better. Maybe talk to and have a friendship, and then we could just see where it goes. I would really like that."

"So, when you meet someone you feel you can trust, someone you feel would care about you for the person that you are, you should hold on to that."

Lochlan smiled, and this one was genuine. "I was thinking the same thing." Their gazes held for a moment. "Do you have a phone?"

Vanessa chuckled. "Everyone has a phone, Loc."

Lochlan rolled her eyes. "One that I can use, please."

Vanessa smiled and handed the phone over. "Are we taking another selfie?"

"Nope." Lochlan was typing something into the phone.

"So, what are we doing?"

Lochlan looked up at her and smiled. "You said when I find someone who cared about me for who I am, to hold to that."

"I did," Vanessa said.

"Then I am holding on to that—to you." She motioned to the phone. "My number is under LP." She waited a beat. "Use it."

"When would you like me to start?"

"Is now too soon?" Lochlan let out the cutest and most nervously adorable laugh that Vanessa had ever heard.

Vanessa lowered her head and smiled. "Why are you trusting me?"

"Because I can't seem not to."

"Thank you." She couldn't seem to look away from Lochlan. It had been a problem all night long. "Good night."

"Good night. Drive safely."

When Vanessa didn't move, they both laughed. "God, I can't seem to move."

"I'm okay with that too. You could just stay there if you'd like."

A horn honked, and Vanessa turned to see Mia standing at their car. "Ugh. I have to go."

"I'll be here a while longer if you want to call or text. I'll get back with you when I can."

"Okay." Vanessa turned to go.

"Oh!" Lochlan said, causing Vanessa to turn once again. "I meant to tell…"

"What?"

"You look really…beautiful."

Vanessa grinned. "Good night, Ms. Paige."

As Vanessa got into the car, Mia spoke. "What was that about?"

"What?"

"Um, because Lochlan never took her eyes off you as you walked to this car. That's what? What just happened?"

"Honestly, I'm not sure."

As they drove away, Mia's brother called and eventually talked them into staying at his house for the night. Mia had gushed over how aware Lochlan was of Vanessa during the entire evening. She had also asked what Lochlan had wanted with Vanessa just before they left. She told Mia that it was just casual and that Lochlan was saying that she was glad that they had been able to come. Vanessa would do as she had been silently asked; she would keep the secret Lochlan had entrusted her with. She loved Mia, but this was too big to ask someone else, especially someone as naturally gabby as Mia, to hold. So, Vanessa would do it herself. She would hold this very special secret for Lochlan until she was ready to deal with it in her own time.

Vanessa sent one text that night explaining that she knew Lochlan was busy and that she and Mia had decided to stay at Mia's brother's home. She explained that if they talked, Mia was sure to ask questions. She regretfully added that she and Lochlan would have to talk another time. Vanessa sighed as she thought back on the conversation and knew that sleep would elude her tonight.

Lochlan looked at her phone for a moment, squinted her eyes in contemplation, and hit send. While she waited on a reply, she packed her things into her bags. She smiled as she heard the notification saying there was a new text. She read the message.

Good morning to you, too. Awake, so you can call if you want.

Lochlan hit the phone icon to place a call. Against Lochlan's better judgment, they had texted a couple of times after Lochlan had left the fundraiser. The messages had stopped, and she had assumed that Vanessa had fallen asleep.

A sleepy voice answered the phone. "Hi."

It was the simplest of words but spoke with such kindness. Lochlan could hear the smile in Vanessa's voice. "Hi."

"Are you heading out?"

"We're loading up, yeah." Lochlan sat back on her bed. "The crew and drivers slept a few hours, so it's back out again. The tour continues."

"So, you'll be in Kansas City tomorrow night?"

Lochlan smiled. "I will be. Sounds like someone is keeping up with my schedule."

"Hey, I'm a big fan these days."

"Am I at Brinley level?"

Vanessa laughed softly. "I'll let you know."

Lochlan took the joke as it was intended. "I can't wait for that moment."

"What about the weather out toward Kansas City?"

"The snow stopped yesterday, and the roads seem to be okay. The amount that St. Louis got caused some damage to the stadium and power supplies, but KC seems to be okay."

"I'm surprised you aren't flying back out."

"I am actually using a different bus until we meet up with mine in Kansas City tonight. I have a friend I write with a lot who's from Knoxville. We're stopping there and picking her up so we can get some writing down for the next album."

"That sounds like a lot of work."

"Yeah, it will take most of the drive, but we both have some things to get down. We're also doing the music sheets for the song I was working on when I got yelled at in a library for being too loud."

Vanessa scoffed. "I did not yell at you!"

"Maybe not, but you very matter-of-factly told me to be quiet."

"You know that I'm going to have to hear that song."

"I thought you already heard it. I vaguely remember the reason I was called down was for singing it too loudly."

Vanessa laughed. "I was studying."

"I remember."

"My parents and I have put a lot of time and money into my brain. I have to make sure it pays off."

"I'm sure that it will. So, what's your major?"

"I'm pre-med. Once I get all my classes done here, I hope to be accepted into Vanderbilt."

Lochlan couldn't help the sudden excitement that she felt about Vanessa attending a college in Nashville. "So, you're moving to Nashville?"

"I hope to eventually, yes. I stayed home because at the time it was the financial thing to do. My dad is a cardiologist, and my mom has a PhD in psychology. They were on board with Vandy, but I think it's crazy to pay that kind of money for my pre-med classes. I'm basically at home and can finish all my classes here, then move on to Vanderbilt when I'm ready to actually start medical school. I just can't see paying sixty-seven thousand a year for math and language classes. Mom's best friend is a nurse anesthetist, and she came out of school with a mound of debt that she paid on for years. My cousin went into the Air Force and they helped with her med school expenses. Medical school is financially exhausting for people, and I don't want that to be my parents or me."

"That's awful. People who are saving lives shouldn't come out of school with hundreds of thousands of dollars' worth of debt."

"Yeah, but that's the way this seems to work."

"Do you have a specialty that you're going into?"

"Pediatric oncology."

"Oh, wow. That's amazing."

"And heartbreaking."

"I can only imagine that it would be."

"Nothing like being surrounded by sick babies and kids." Vanessa's tone became somber.

"That would be a hard one to pick." Vanessa didn't say anything for a moment, making Loc wonder if there was more to the choice than she'd said. "Can I ask you something?"

"Sure."

"Is there a reason you chose that in particular?" Vanessa didn't answer for a moment, and Lochlan heard the intake of her breath. "You don't have to tell me if—"

"My little brother Michael died when he was seven."

A pain shot through Lochlan. "I'm so sorry."

"My parents spent a lot of time at Vanderbilt with Michael. My brother Chris and I were never allowed to go when Michael had treatments. They tried to keep it from us for a while, but we always knew that Michael was in the hospital when we would stay with our grandparents for a weekend. Looking back on it now, and knowing how awful treatments are, I understand why they shielded us from that."

"Is that why it's Vandy for you?"

"I guess. Vanderbilt is one of the top hospitals, but yeah, maybe Michael has more to do with it than I allow myself to believe. I just want to help kids like him. I was young, and I couldn't help him then, but maybe I can save someone else's Michael."

"How old were you?"

"Eleven. Chris was nine." Lochlan hated the sadness in Vanessa's voice. "My parents almost didn't get over it. My mom was a practicing therapist at the time, and she couldn't even deal with her own grief. She took three years off after his death. She hovered over me and Chris to the point my grandparents had to step in and talk her into getting some help herself."

"That must have been awful for all of you."

"It was, but in the long run, it made us closer—stronger. Mom has a more insightful view of her patients that lose children now. Michael gave her a unique perspective."

"And because of Michael, you will help a lot of kids."

"I hope so." Vanessa paused a moment. "So, what about you? Siblings?"

"Two brothers and a sister. Brothers are older, and my sister, Kayla, is younger." There was a knock on Lochlan's door. "Come in."

Jamie stuck her head in the door. "Hey, Loc, we're pulling out in fifteen. You ready?"

"Yeah, I'll be right down." Once Jamie left the room, Lochlan went back to her call. "Hey."

"I heard." Vanessa laughed quietly.

"Why are you being so quiet?"

"Mia is still sleeping, but I thought I heard someone outside the door. Hell, it's six forty-five."

"I'm surprised that she didn't want to talk to me too." Lochlan laughed.

"She doesn't know I'm talking to you."

"Why not?"

"I love her, but she tends to have loose lips sometimes, especially when she's drinking."

"There you are protecting me again."

"Just seems to be something I do."

"I kinda like it."

"Me too. I like that you see me differently from the other people you meet."

"And I do." She took a deep breath, "Okay. I gotta go."

"Have a safe trip."

"You too. Will you text me when you and Mia are home today?"

"I can."

"I would like that." Lochlan stood and retrieved her bag. "All right, I'm heading out."

"And away from me."

"Seems so." Lochlan thought a moment. "Hey, I'll be in Charlotte in August. What are my chances of talking you into coming to an amazing concert?"

"What? Is Brinley coming with you?"

Lochlan gasped. "Ouch."

Vanessa laughed. "I would love to see you in concert. Outside of that acoustic set you did at the fundraiser, I haven't seen you perform."

"Ouch, again." She heard Vanessa laughing. "I normally don't have to try this hard." Lochlan stopped and tried to backtrack. "I mean with people…I normally don't have—"

Vanessa was laughing again. "I understand what you meant."

Lochlan stepped out of her hotel room and saw Jamie tapping her foot impatiently. "Right, I have to go. Text me later."

"I will."

"Bye." As Lochlan put her phone into her pocket, Jamie was looking at her inquisitively. "It was Kayla," Lochlan said. And in that moment, where she and Vanessa were both lying to their best friends, she knew things were about to get tricky.

CHAPTER FOUR

Lochlan felt her phone buzzing in her pocket and smiled as she answered it. "Hey." Jamie turned to Lochlan in question.

"Hey. What are you doing right now?"

Lochlan smiled. "I am currently walking over the Michigan Avenue Bridge in Chicago." Lochlan stopped walking, obviously hoping for privacy.

"I love that place. Oh my God, are they turning the water green for St. Patrick's Day?" Vanessa asked.

"They did. It's the first time that I've been in the area during March, so I told everyone that I wanted to see it."

"Well, I'll let you go. I was just going to tell you that they played the new song on the radio just now."

Lochlan swelled with pride. "And? What did you think?"

"Are you kidding? Your voice is amazing. The song is very catchy and is a good pre-summer upbeat song."

"I'm glad that you like it."

"I do. So, what are your plans for today?"

"We just came from the amazing aquarium that they have here, then we went by the stadium to check things out. So now we're here looking at the water."

"Should you be on the streets like that?"

"It's a cooler day, so I'm dressed in layers, have on a ball cap and sunglasses. I really don't think anyone is paying attention to me. Everyone is taking in the scenery."

"Then I'll let you get back to what you are doing. Just wanted to tell you they played the new song."

"That's all?" Lochlan teased her.

"Okay, so maybe I missed talking to you. It's been three days."

"I know. I've been scheduled for a lot here."

"How was the baseball game?"

"It was fun. Preseason games are still games and the Braves won, so it was a good day."

"I saw the pictures on Instagram of you in your Braves shirt. That had to make a good impression on Wrigley Field." Vanessa laughed.

"It wasn't like I showed up in a White Sox shirt. There would have been hell to pay for that. The Braves are the closest thing that Tennessee has ever had to a pro baseball team. My fans get it."

"Okay, go do your thing, superstar."

"It may be late when I'm done tonight, but I'll call back maybe tomorrow once we're back on the road."

"Sounds good. Have a good show."

"Thanks."

Jamie approached Lochlan as she ended the call. "Everything okay?"

Lochlan knew that was Jamie code for asking who the caller was, but Lochlan wasn't in the mood to hear a lecture, so she vaguely answered, "Yeah, everything's fine," as she walked around Jamie, working to ignore that hard stare she received.

❖

Lochlan laughed as she looked up at the ceiling of her tour bus. "You get that this is an impossible question, right?" she said to Vanessa, who was on FaceTime.

"No, it isn't." Vanessa joined her in a burst of laughter.

"This isn't easy."

"It's just a question. Who is your favorite queer character?"

"Okay." Lochlan sat up straight. "Mayor Mills," Lochlan said of her television character girl crush from the series *Once Upon a Time.*

Vanessa gasped. "You can't pick her. She isn't a queer character, no matter how much we all know she should have been. Stick to the rules. You can't pick Regina Mills."

"Ugh." Lochlan moaned. "But she is my favorite."

"I meant a character who is actually out."

"It's not my fault the writers didn't listen to all the fans. That's on them. She is my pick."

"Okay, okay. You can pick her." Vanessa asked the next question. "Favorite movie?"

"I feel as though you are going to judge me when I say *Jaws.*"

"I don't even know why I'm playing this game with you."

"Because I'm stuck in this house on wheels as we're going down the interstate and you feel sorry for me. You know that I need you to keep me company."

"Oh, yeah, that."

"I am rarely on this bus alone. It's so quiet."

"Well, at least Jamie isn't around to ask you questions or order you to get off the phone."

Loc winced, but she couldn't deny that Jamie's absence made it much easier to talk freely to Vanessa. "Yes, let's be thankful that it's Eli's birthday and she needed to go home."

"Everyone needs to be home on their birthday."

Lochlan was quiet a moment. "I don't remember the last one I spent at home."

"That's awful."

"Yeah, it's not far from Christmas so I'm usually off doing some Christmas special somewhere."

"December fourth. It's marked on my calendar."

"Did you google me?"

"Maybe."

Lochlan laughed. "Since I can't just pull up Wikipedia and learn yours, when is it?"

"April twenty-fourth," Vanessa answered.

"Wow, that's just a few weeks away."

"It is."

Lochlan grabbed her tablet and entered the date into her calendar. "Will you go home?"

"Not sure. I assume I'll see my family at some point. Mom always calls me at the exact time I was born."

Lochlan made an "aww" sound. "That is so sweet."

"Loc, I was born at seven fourteen a.m. It doesn't feel sweet at seven fourteen a.m."

"Still sweet," Lochlan insisted as she tried to hide her yawn.

"Okay, you need some rest."

"Probably. I'm not as hardcore as med students."

"We all have our demons."

"Call me tomorrow?" Lochlan asked.

"I can. I'm having lunch with Mia and Ty, but after that, you're on."

"It's a date." Lochlan realized what she had said, "I mean—"

"It's a date." Vanessa agreed.

"I look forward to it." Lochlan yawned again. "Okay, I unfortunately can't keep my eyes open any longer."

"Good night, Lochlan. Sleep well."

As Lochlan ended the FaceTime chat, she thought about what a date with Vanessa would feel like. What they would do? Where they would go? She thought about what she knew of Vanessa and what things she might enjoy. Just before sleep claimed her, Lochlan had a perfect idea.

❖

Vanessa woke to the ringing of her phone. "Hello," she answered groggily.

"Happy birthday, sweetheart."

Vanessa smiled. "Hi, Mom." She looked over at her clock that read 7:14 a.m. "Sometimes I wish I was born at noon."

Her mother laughed. "Well, I wish you had been born during the evening. That way I didn't have to be in labor for sixteen hours, but here we are."

Vanessa was grateful that her mom's tone was playful. "For that, I answer the phone every year at seven fourteen. It's like my gift to you, Mom."

"Do you know what a wonderful gift to me would be?" Vanessa knew what was coming next. "To see my baby this weekend."

It was Friday, so Vanessa still had a few classes to attend this morning. "How about I meet you for dinner tonight?"

"Is that all the time you have?"

Vanessa smiled at the reality of the situation. She couldn't tell her mother that just last night she received a text from Lochlan that said simply, *Do you trust me?* When she had replied *Yes*, a message came to her with a link. A link to an airline ticket and directions to board the plane in Charlotte. A car would be awaiting her arrival at the airport in Indianapolis. She had no clue what Lochlan was up to but was aware Lochlan was playing in Indianapolis this weekend. She remembered there was a question that her mother had asked. "I have plans with friends tomorrow night, so I need to be back here in the morning."

"So, you're squeezing me in tonight?" Her mother mocked hurt. "I guess I'll take it."

"Good, I really miss you guys."

"Well, the feeling is definitely mutual. Your dad and I thought when you went to school less than an hour from home that we would see you more, but we understand you took a full load to finish up your prerequisite courses."

"Yeah, busy, busy."

"So, what do your friends have planned this weekend?"

Vanessa smiled. "I honestly have no idea. It's a surprise of some kind."

"Oh, that's nice. It says a lot about someone when they take the time to surprise you like that."

At the thought, Vanessa's heart skipped a beat. "Yes, it does."

"Well then, I'll let you rest a bit more before class. Your brother is joining us for dinner."

"Aww, great. I miss Chris."

"I know that you do. Can you at least stay the night?"

Since her flight wasn't until noon, and she was flying out of Charlotte, which was a short drive from her parents' house, she answered, "Sure, Mom. I just need to head back around ten in the morning."

"Wonderful. We'll have both of you under one roof tonight."

"I look forward to it. My last class ends at one." She looked over at the bag that she already had packed for her flight to Indianapolis. "So, I'll have everything together and ready to leave once class is done."

"That will put you here around two?"

"Yeah."

"All right. Your dad is leaving the office shortly after lunch and I won't be far behind him. Chris came in last night, so he'll be here when you arrive."

"Sounds good." There was a knock at the door. "Hey, Mom, someone is at the door."

"At seven thirty in the morning?"

"*You* called at seven fourteen."

"And I am your mother, who gave birth to you at that ungodly hour."

Vanessa smiled as she went to the door. "Bye, Mom."

"Bye, sweetheart. Love you."

"You too. See you tonight." Vanessa looked through the peephole to only see balloons.

She opened the door to a young delivery guy. "Are you Vanessa Wallace?"

"I am." He handed her the balloons and an envelope as she thanked his retreating form.

Once inside her room, she looked at the multicolored balloons, with one larger balloon that read Happy Birthday. She opened the card.

You will be delivered tomorrow afternoon to the hotel listed. Here is your check-in information once you arrive, which should be around 1:30. I will be waiting for your call then. Happy birthday and I hope you have a wonderful day.—Loc

Vanessa smiled at the card. *Is this really happening to me?*

❖

"Happy birthday." Vanessa's father hugged her.

"Thanks, Daddy."

As soon as he let her go, she was engulfed in another bear hug. "Happy birthday, sis."

"Thank you." She hugged her brother tightly. "Oh, I've missed you."

"You too," he said sincerely.

"Go ahead and put your things away," her dad said. "Your mom will be here shortly."

Chris reached for the bag. "I got that." He walked alongside Vanessa to her childhood room. "How's school?"

"Good. And you?"

"Good," he replied. "Sorry I didn't get a chance to call you back last week."

"I'm sure that you're busy with all the ladies in Chapel Hill."

"I am." He smiled. "And speaking of all the ladies, anything new I need to hear? Any of the women in Raleigh looking to make an honest woman out of my big sister?"

"Your big sister isn't looking for a woman at the moment. She is merely trying to survive school."

"You being BFFs with Lochlan Paige had to help with the ladies."

Vanessa threw a pillow at him. "I am not BFFs with anyone."

He caught the pillow and began a hearty laugh. "Oh my God. You are blushing."

Vanessa felt horrified. "I am not."

"You are! You are blushing." He sat on her bed. "That picture was months ago."

"Yes, it was. And it was also the last of its kind."

"But you're blushing."

"Lochlan Paige is a very famous woman, who happens to

be beautiful. I am a lesbian, in case you've forgotten, so yes, I guess I have a small celebrity crush."

"Okay. I guess that when you're ready to tell me, you will."

He stood. "Chris—" He stopped and looked down at her. "There is nothing to tell."

"Mia texted me yesterday. Said your friends had hoped to surprise you with a birthday party tomorrow night. Asked if I could try to change your mind about not coming back to Raleigh and that I need to give her a call if I could." He watched as she started to play with her hands. "So, imagine my surprise when Mom tells me that you have to head back tomorrow morning to meet up with your friends." When there was no response, he added, "So, they think you're here, while Mom thinks that you're going back to be with your friends. You get that I have caught you in a lie, right?"

"Chris—"

"You don't have to tell me. I just want to be here for you. I told neither Mom nor Mia what I knew, and I won't, but if you need to talk, I'm here. I'm on your side and your secrets have always been safe with me."

Chris had been the first person Vanessa had told she was gay. He had kept her secret for two years without breathing a word of it to anyone. She also knew that amongst his friends, Chris was the one you could tell anything that needed to be guarded.

Just before he was about to walk out the door, the words rushed out. "I'm flying to Indianapolis tomorrow to meet Lochlan. We've been talking for a couple of months and if anyone found out—it's her career, Chris."

He didn't have a chance to speak before her mom came into the room. "Hello, sweetheart."

Vanessa stood to meet her mother in an embrace. "Hi,

Mom." She held her mother tightly and looked over her shoulder to mouth her brother the words "Please" and "Shhh."

Chris nodded and left.

❖

Lochlan's intern assistant entered her hotel suite. "Ms. Paige. You wanted to see me?"

Lochlan looked up at her and replied with a smile. "I did, Spencer." She motioned for her to have a seat. "I have something that I need for you to handle tomorrow."

"Sure."

"This is your own special project. I need this to be done precisely as I tell you, and I need to know that I can trust you to do that."

"I will do my absolute best, Ms. Paige."

Jamie had always spoken highly of Spencer's organizational skills, so Lochlan felt fairly confident in handing this off to her."My driver will take you to the airport tomorrow at one, where you will meet my friend Vanessa. She will be flying in from Charlotte, and you will escort her back to this hotel." Lochlan handed her a room key. "This room, two doors down from mine, belongs to her. You will see Vanessa to her room, let her get situated, and when that is done, you and the driver will bring her to the stadium. I have sound check at two, so you will bring her in and around to the stage."

"I can do that," Spencer said. "Your friend must be very excited to see you in concert."

"I hope so. Anything outside of the concert will be a surprise to her, so you'll need to do as I ask without informing her of any plans." Lochlan smiled. "This weekend, you will oversee everything having to do with Vanessa. If she needs anything, you get it. Understood?"

"Yes, ma'am."

"It's Vanessa's birthday weekend, so I want my friend to have a good time."

"I understand." Spencer nodded. "I will take care of it."

"Also, later this evening you will receive a text from this number." Lochlan handed her a piece of paper. "You will meet a guy named Corbin. Corbin will have an envelope for you."

"Okay." Spencer seemed intrigued. "This all seems so exciting."

Lochlan smiled as she hoped Vanessa felt the same way. "When you get the envelope, you contact me and I'll take it from you."

"I won't let you down. Your friend will have an amazing time."

Lochlan smiled back. "Thank you. That's all."

"I'm on it." She left the room.

Lochlan sighed as the reality set in. She was actually going to try to woo Vanessa. She felt a mixture of excitement and nerves. "Okay. Here we go."

❖

Vanessa had an amazing time with her family. Her parents had taken her and Chris to the family's favorite Italian restaurant. They had laughed about things that were going on with them at school. Chris had met a girl a couple of months ago that he was interested in. That, of course, prompted questions from her parents, asking Vanessa if she had found a nice girl. After glancing quickly at Chris, she simply replied that she was very busy with her studies.

When the sun came up the next morning, she wiped at her

eyes as she stretched. She reached over to check the time when she saw the text alert. She clicked on the icon and smiled when she saw the message.

I'll be busy when you arrive, but my assistant, Spencer, will meet you at the airport and take you to your destinations. I'll meet the two of you at the stadium where I'm playing tonight. Can't wait to see you. Hope you had a good time with the family.

She forced herself out of bed and went down to have breakfast with her family. Her parents hated to see the time come for Vanessa to have to leave. They hugged her good-bye and told her to be careful going back to Raleigh.

Chris helped her load her bags into the car. "Okay, you're ready to head out. Can I ask what your plans are?"

"I fly out at noon, so I need to get to the airport. Other than seeing the concert, I honestly don't know."

"Is this serious?"

Vanessa laughed at the fact he was honestly expecting an answer that she hadn't figured out herself. "I don't know, Chris. As serious as it can be between two people who have been in a room together only twice. We've spent more time just talking over FaceTime and text messages than we have been face-to-face."

"So, you've only seen her twice?"

"Today will be the third time."

"And she's flying you there?" He chuckled. "Wow."

"I think that she's so used to people wanting her for who she is, that when she meets someone who makes her feel that she isn't just Lochlan Paige, she wants to be around that person."

"And that's you? She wants to be around you?"

"She's flying me to Indy, so…"

He laughed. "I can't believe that you're having this hidden thing with Lochlan freaking Paige." He shook his head. "What is she like?"

"Amazing." Vanessa smiled. "She is beautiful and funny, and she is so sweet."

"That's all I need to know."

"Chris…" Vanessa became serious. "You know you can't tell anyone about this. This is her career. No one can know."

"I got it." He pulled her into a hug. "She's hot and famous, but you're my sister. You're the one I'll do this for."

"Thank you." She hugged him tightly. She was quiet a moment. "I told her about Michael."

He pulled back. "You never talk about Mike." Since their brother's death, Vanessa had been the most closed-off about him.

"We talked about school and my specialty. He just came up."

"It's good that you talked to her. You must trust her." He took in her disposition. "I think you trust her even more than you know."

Vanessa sighed. "Look at us. We're trusting each other with the things that we hold the dearest."

"You better get on the road. You gotta get through security."

"I do." Vanessa smiled.

"I would tell you to send Lochlan a hello for me, but…"

"Right," Vanessa answered. "Secret and all."

"Sweet Lord, my sister is dating Lochlan Paige."

Vanessa didn't argue at the term, only smiling as she got into the car. "See ya later."

❖

Vanessa's trip had gone smoothly. She had exited the terminal and saw a very bubbly redhead at baggage claim holding a sign that read *Ms. Wallace*. She walked over to her. "I'm Vanessa. I assume I'm with you?"

"You are. My name is Spencer." She took the rolling luggage from Vanessa. "I work for your friend." Spencer seemed careful not to mention names in the crowd of people. "We have an SUV just outside that will take us to the hotel."

"Great."

"Is this your first trip to Indy?"

"It is, yes."

"Well, you'll have an exciting night." As they approached the SUV, a man exited and took the luggage from them and placed it in the back. Spencer spoke again as they entered the vehicle. "I'm sure that you're excited to see your friend in concert as well."

"I am. This will be my first."

Spencer's mouth fell open. "You've never seen her in concert?"

"Not a full show, no." Vanessa squinted in embarrassment.

"Oh, you're in for such a treat. I've seen her perform every weekend for three months now. I also have seen her twice just as a fan. She is amazing in concert."

"I assume she is."

"She isn't the highest-selling concert ticket for no reason," Spencer said proudly.

"I imagine not." Vanessa smiled at Spencer, who seemed to be fangirling right before her eyes. "Well, you've made me even more excited now."

Spencer seemed giddy for her. "I'll take you to your room and let you put your things down, then we'll head over to sound check where Ms. Paige is waiting."

"Sounds good."

Vanessa was shown to her room. As they passed one of the rooms, Spencer spoke. "That's Ms. Paige's room there." Vanessa looked at the door. "I'm sure that she'll go over all that with you later." As they arrived two doors down, Spencer placed the key card in the door. "Here we are."

Vanessa walked into the room trying to hide her surprise, but her mouth dropped open slightly as she slowly took in the space before her. Damn, this wasn't a typical hotel room. In fact, she was pretty sure that she could have fit their whole apartment in the sitting room of the suite. She went to the window and looked out over the city. She couldn't help but wonder what in the hell she was doing here, and why Loc had taken to her so easily.

Vanessa's thoughts were interrupted by the voice beside her. "It's an amazing view, right?" Spencer said as she placed Vanessa's luggage in the bedroom.

"It is."

"Did you notice it?"

Vanessa was puzzled. "Notice what?"

Spencer smiled. "I guess not." She joined her at the window and pointed slightly to the left. "There's the stadium."

Vanessa smiled as she saw the large stadium front, but her smile grew wider as she saw the billboard that faced her hotel. Amongst the changing pictures of upcoming events at the stadium, Lochlan's picture came up. She was standing, the flawless legs that she was known for slightly spread. Her head was thrown back, mic inches from her mouth as she apparently was hitting the high pitch-perfect note, with her other hand on top of a mic stand. There was a pink banner running diagonally across the bottom of the picture that read, Sold Out. She turned to Spencer. "I think I'm about to get really excited."

They both laughed. "Okay. Sound check started about fifteen minutes ago. We can either head over now, or we can wait for a moment."

Vanessa was brought back to reality and the fact that she had been up since eight this morning, been through two airports, and it was now just after two in the afternoon. "I would like to freshen up before we go."

"Of course." Spencer smiled. "I'll just wait for you here."

Vanessa returned the smile and went into the bedroom, closing the door behind her. She took out her phone and snapped a picture of the room, the likes of which she had only ever seen in magazines. She attached the photo to a message.

Chris, you have to see this room. This is JUST the bedroom. Flight went well. About to head to the stadium.

She went to the bathroom to reapply makeup and try to make her hair presentable. She was casually dressed but had made sure that she looked nice just in case she saw Lochlan before she had a chance to change. Her phone buzzed on the vanity.

Damn it, sis. You're sleeping with her, aren't you?

She laughed and could almost hear her brother doing the same as she typed the reply.

No, I have not.

Just before she and Spencer left the room, her phone buzzed again. She laughed at the reply from Chris.

Maybe I should ask you that question again on Monday?

❖

Vanessa and Spencer entered the back of the stadium and walked down the hallway. The halls were half occupied by the large rolling boxes that were used to transport the equipment for the bands and crew. They had been walking for quite a while when she saw an opening that showed the corner of the stage. There was no music at first, but just as they approached, she heard Lochlan laugh. "Okay, let's try that disaster again. I'll try to remember the words this time."

Just then, she and Spencer cleared the dock opening and she was looking at the back side of Lochlan. She saw her walk across the stage and over to the ramp that led to the risers of the stadium. She was singing a song that Vanessa knew well. It was one of the songs that had been released on Lochlan's first album and was one that had climbed the chart to number one in record-breaking speed. Lochlan tapped her foot to the music and then descended the corner of the stage. She then crossed the main stage and out the walkway that extended to the middle of the floor seating area. Lochlan stopped at the end of the walkway and belted out the notes. She turned to head back down the walkway and then came their way and climbed the corner ramp to stage left. She continued to sing for a moment, then turned to make her way back to center stage. As she turned, her eyes met Vanessa's. Her voice caught for a second but picked right back up. She smiled and waved slightly, using only her fingers.

Vanessa returned the gesture. "Okay, she knows that you're here," Spencer said and turned and started to walk away. "Come with me, please."

Vanessa was sad that she was leaving, as it felt like she had just gotten here. "Where are we going?"

"First off, I am not letting you see any more until tonight. I don't want to ruin it for you."

The farther they walked, the quieter Loc's voice became. Within a moment, they were in an elevator going to the first level. When the doors opened, she could hear the music again. They were walking through the level where people were working to open concessions for this evening. They slowed just in front of a long table and Spencer smiled at the woman behind it. "Hey, Jess."

"Hey ya, Spencer."

"This is Vanessa. She's a good friend of Ms. Paige and it's her first concert, so we need some things for her." As Vanessa eyed the assortment of items ranging from DVDs to key chains, Spencer said, "Get me a cap and a program, and let her pick a shirt."

Vanessa studied the shirts on display. She was quickly drawn to the one adorned with the picture that was on the billboard outside her hotel room. It was those damned legs. "I'll take one of those." As Jess handed her the shirt, Vanessa smiled. "Thank you."

"Any time, dear. If you need anything else, you just come back up."

Vanessa took the bag. "I think that should do it."

She followed Spencer to the elevator and down the lower level hallway where they had been earlier. "Here we are."

Spencer knocked on the door, and when there wasn't a sound, she opened it. The large room had two couches, a makeup mirror that was covered with lights, and two vases of flowers sitting on a table in the center of the room. "Lochlan will be done in about twenty minutes. You can wait for her here. I'll be just outside if you need me." She pointed to the table in the corner. "There are some treats and fruit on the table. The cooler just beside it is also full of drinks of any kind. The beer company that is one of the sponsors always has a large assortment of options, but Ms. Paige doesn't drink, so help yourself. There are also sodas and water. You're welcome to anything that's there."

"Thank you," Vanessa said as she made her way to one of the couches.

"You're welcome. If you need me, just let me know." With that, Spencer left the room.

Vanessa sat on the couch and went through the program that she had in the bag. She loved the cute pictures from Lochlan's childhood. She was in awe of the young girl the photos showed standing on a stage in a Knoxville talent show. It was at that talent show that Lochlan had been discovered. Even at a young age, Lochlan was beautiful. There were photos of the Country Music Association awards that she had won multiple times. Photos of her Grammy wins over the past twelve years, and red carpet appearances with some of the most attractive men in the entertainment business. Out of nowhere, Vanessa started humming the song that she had heard Lochlan singing earlier. She was flipping through the pages, reading the bio when she heard the door to the dressing room open.

"Oh God, please don't look at those horrendous baby pictures."

Vanessa looked up to see Lochlan. "I think they're adorable."

Lochlan stood just inside the door. "Hi." She smiled.

"Hi."

She sat beside Vanessa. "How was the flight?"

"Great. No issues."

"Good." Lochlan glanced over at the book in her hands. "Reading my bio?"

"I am." Vanessa smiled. "Amazing the things you can learn about a person. I think everyone should carry one of these things around with them."

Lochlan took the book and put it back in the bag. "Tell you what, I have some food waiting for us at the hotel. Come eat dinner with me and I'll tell you anything that you want to know about me." Lochlan stood and Vanessa followed.

"Food sounds great. I'm starving."

Just then there was a knock at the door and Jamie came in. "Hey, Loc—" Jamie stopped when she saw Vanessa. A flash of confusion showed briefly in her eyes before her professional demeanor returned.

"Jamie, this is Vanessa Wallace." Lochlan turned to Vanessa. "Vanessa, this is Jamie Holt. She is my right hand. My fixer of all things. I couldn't do this without her."

Vanessa could tell the smile on Jamie's face was forced. To be Lochlan's fixer of all things, she seemed very surprised to see Vanessa. After a moment, Jamie spoke. "It's nice to finally meet you."

"You too," Vanessa responded.

"We're heading over to the hotel for an early dinner."

Jamie looked at her watch. "It's three now, Loc. I need you back here by six."

"Got it," Lochlan said as she picked up her bag. "I'll be at the hotel relaxing, so if you need me, that's where I'll be." Jamie seemed to accept Lochlan's unspoken message. Vanessa assumed it was Lochlan's polite way of saying she was done with the conversation.

Chapter Five

Lochlan and Vanessa entered a hotel room that featured a beautifully decorated table in the center of the room. Ornate place settings, sparkling utensils, and a vase of fresh flowers stood on a spotless white tablecloth. Lochlan picked up the phone and spoke into it. "Yes. This is room 1504. We're ready for dinner." She returned the phone to its receiver after a quick "thank you." She turned to Vanessa, who stood in front the window. "It's a good view."

Vanessa turned to her. "It is." She smiled. "I love that billboard, by the way."

"Thank you." She joined Vanessa at the window just as the picture showed. "They love the legs."

"Because they're really good legs."

Lochlan chuckled. "Thank you. I now approve of the billboard that plays just outside your window." She turned to Vanessa. "So, is that the reason that you picked that shirt? You like my legs?"

Vanessa blushed and was saved by a knock at the door, as someone said, "Room service."

"That would be dinner." Lochlan allowed the man in. He took the items off the cart and set them on the table. "There you are, Ms. Paige. If you would like anything else, don't hesitate to let us know."

"Thank you." She handed the man a tip and showed him to the door.

"That looks too good to even eat."

Lochlan smiled. "Well, I hope that isn't going to stop you. We're both starving, and I have a long night ahead of me." She motioned for Vanessa to have a seat.

"Thank you, Ms. Paige." Lochlan smiled slightly, but Vanessa could tell that something was wrong. "What?"

"Lochlan Paige is who I am to people who only know me at a certain level. My full name is Lochlan Paige Westbrook. I don't want you to be one of those people who only know Lochlan Paige."

Vanessa smiled. "I hope that I'm not."

"You're not." Lochlan blushed. "So how was the birthday?"

"It was good, but getting better, Ms. Westbrook." Lochlan smiled at the change. "I got to spend some much-needed time with my parents and Chris."

"I love that you're close to them."

"Yeah, me too. I see so many people who have families who are no more than distant acquaintances. Tell me about your brothers. You've mentioned your sister, Kayla, during conversations, but not your brothers as much."

"Brad is an accountant for a tax firm in Knoxville. He's a great guy and still single. Kyle is the oldest. He and his wife are the proud parents of my adorable nephew, Casey. Kyle and Jane own a real estate agency in Knoxville. Like you said, you already know about Kayla. She's a senior at the University of Tennessee."

"Does your fame affect them?"

Lochlan laughed. "No. They think I'm a geek. They don't understand why anyone would want my autograph or a picture with me. They love me, but my fame is something they like to give me hell about. When someone says, 'She's your sister?'

they always say, 'Yes, and she's still that annoying kid we grew up with.'"

Vanessa laughed. "They sound fun."

"They are. They keep me grounded and we all appreciate that. That's why I feel so comfortable with you. To you, I'm just me."

"Of course you are. Now, when I see that mega country star tonight, I don't know about her."

Lochlan blushed. "Thanks for the heads-up."

Vanessa pushed her food around. "I have to say, I'm pretty excited."

"Well then, I'll give it my best. Normally, I just have to impress thousands of people during a show, but tonight I have to impress them *and* a girl." Lochlan smiled. "But no pressure."

"Just worry about the thousands." Vanessa gestured around the room. "You have already impressed the girl."

Lochlan beamed. "So you like the birthday getaway?"

"I get to see you, so yeah, I would say it's a win. Getting to see Lochlan Paige in concert is merely a bonus."

"Which is a very good answer. I also have a gift for you that you'll get later tonight." Vanessa raised an eyebrow. "Dirty mind," Lochlan said. "It's not that."

"Well, that's unfortunate."

Lochlan broke the awkward silence. "So, I'll take you to work with me tonight, and then you'll get your other gifts."

"Gifts? As in plural?"

"As in, you'll have to wait until later."

Vanessa smiled. "Thank you so much for this. You didn't have to, but I have to say it's nice being whisked away and shown a different side of you."

Lochlan sobered. "Most people would think the side of me that I've shown you is the different side to me."

"Loc, to me you're the girl I met in a library. The girl who texts me a good night message almost every night. The one I share things with on a crazy day like, 'Hey, my lab partner almost killed us all today.' This…" She looked around. "It's nice, but to me"—she motioned between them—"this is who you are to me." Vanessa smiled. "Now, when I see you tonight, that voice, that stage presence"—she raised her eyebrow—"those million-dollar legs on full display, only then will I see another side to you. But for me, this is the only you that I want to see."

Lochlan winced. "Maybe having you see Lochlan Paige is a bad idea."

Vanessa shrugged. "I don't know. She's kinda hot."

Lochlan chucked. "Thanks?"

At just after six, Lochlan and Vanessa were driven into the stadium. When they got out, Vanessa got another look at Lochlan Paige, the country music star. As the passenger door was opened and dozens of people met them, the Loc she knew was gone. Immediately, there was a chorus of voices, with Jamie's the loudest of all. "Loc, we need to do meet and greets before the band starts. You were supposed to have been here half an hour ago."

"Sorry, but I'm here now."

Very few people even noticed that anyone was with Lochlan. Vanessa watched as she walked away quickly, followed closely by the group of people. They were all asking questions about what Lochlan needed or wanted. She was answering questions in rapid-fire. She suddenly stopped, causing an assistant to almost run into the back of her. She turned quickly. "Where is Vanessa?" She looked over the people. The crowd of Lochlan Paige's minions turned toward Spencer and Vanessa. Lochlan moved to where they were standing. "Give me a second."

"Loc—"

"I said, give me a second." Lochlan cut Jamie off.

Lochlan took Vanessa by the arm and led her away from Spencer and out of earshot. "Hey. Sorry about that." Vanessa saw it, that faint frown. "Like I told you, here, to them, I'm Lochlan Paige, and sometimes things get really hectic."

"It's okay. I get that it's take your friend to work day."

"Yeah." The smile returned to Loc's face. "Things are about to get crazy in there. Everyone will insist on a piece of my time until I hit that stage. Then, when I step off that stage, it starts again. During that time, I want you to understand that I'll try my best to acknowledge that you're here."

Vanessa laughed. "It's okay. Really. Maybe this is something I need to see. Something that will help me understand the girl who hides between bookshelves in a library."

"Thank you." She turned to the group. "It's game time." She went with Vanessa back toward Spencer. "Spencer?"

"Yes, Ms. Paige?"

"You understand your role tonight?"

"Yes, ma'am. Tonight, Ms. Wallace is my responsibility. Anything she wants or needs, I make sure it happens."

"Perfect." Lochlan smiled at Vanessa. "Okay, welcome to Lochlan Paige's world." With that, Lochlan rejoined the group of people who awaited the woman who, in many ways, Vanessa would meet for the first time tonight—Lochlan Paige.

❖

At 7:45, Spencer and Vanessa were walking around the first level of the stadium. They weaved in and out of concertgoers, looked at the other band's merchandise, and grabbed a couple of sodas. Spencer had explained that Lochlan was with Jamie, finishing up meet and greets from the fan club. Then she would return to her dressing room where she would go through her vocal warm-ups. They went to find their seats, which were located just to the right of the stage.

Vanessa watched the throngs of people who were so excited to see Lochlan. She couldn't help but smile and somehow feel a sense of pride. When her phone buzzed, she smiled as she saw the sender's name.

Hey, where are you?

Vanessa quickly replied.

We're up on the first level. About to head to our seats.

She waited until the reply message came in.

Okay. Tell Spencer to bring you back down once the band is done. I'll have a minute before I need to go out.
Will do. See you in a bit.

Vanessa tucked her phone back in her jeans just before she and Spencer descended the stairs to their seats. They were on the third row, just to the corner of the stage. Vanessa had never thought about how good seats like that would be. As the lights dimmed, the crowd cheered. They settled in and watched the warm-up band. The group did an amazing job, and she and Spencer sang and danced to the hits.

After a final bow and good night from the opening act, Vanessa and Spencer quickly made their way to the elevator. Jamie was standing guard outside the dressing room, and she firmly indicated they should wait until Lochlan finished the ritual pre-show meeting with her band. Soon, the door opened, and several people left the room. Jamie stuck her head in, said something that Vanessa couldn't hear, then moved, motioning with her head for Vanessa to go in.

She walked in, and the door closed behind her. What Vanessa saw surprised her. Lochlan was pacing the room, shaking her hands out and humming loudly to keep her voice warm. "Hey."

She stopped and looked up at Vanessa. "Hey."

Vanessa's heart stopped, and her mouth went completely dry at the vision that stood before her. Lochlan looked incredible. She had on knee-high boots with a black skirt that clung to her toned thighs. Her shirt was slightly oversized and white. Her hair was flawless, and her makeup was something that an artist had done. Lochlan laughed, bringing Vanessa back to the present.

"Sorry," Vanessa said as she blushed.

"I've been looked at a lot of ways, but that's now my favorite one."

"Is it weird that now I see the other Lochlan Paige? The beautiful, flawless, Lochlan Paige?"

Lochlan's smile fell. "That depends on how you still feel about Lochlan Westbrook."

"Honestly?" Lochlan nodded. "I still see you, Loc. You are just really…" Vanessa slightly shook her head. "God, you are gorgeous."

Lochlan's smile returned. "Okay. I can deal with this version winning for now."

There was a knock at the door and Jamie leaned in. "Vanessa, you need to make your way to your seat if you want to see her come out. And trust me when I say, you want to see that."

"Thanks." Vanessa nodded as Jamie closed the door, relieved that she had been somewhat friendly.

"So, where are the seats?" Lochlan asked. "That way I know where you are."

"Third row to the right of the stage."

"Stage left. Got it."

"Okay, I think I should go out."

"Yeah."

"You seem nervous."

Lochlan smiled weakly. "Still worried about impressing the girl."

Vanessa took a chance and stepped forward. She leaned in, then stopped as she gestured to Lochlan. "I don't want to mess anything up."

Lochlan swallowed hard. "I have people who can fix anything you're about to do."

Vanessa placed the slightest of kisses to her cheek and whispered, "I am very impressed by any version that I have seen of you. Relax."

Lochlan stood stone still and only turned her eyes watching Vanessa back away. "Yeah, that helped."

Vanessa laughed with her. "Sorry."

When they were outside the room with Lochlan's band, Vanessa turned to her one last time. "I'll see you when you're done."

Vanessa rejoined Spencer at the elevator and took it back to the first level. They were in their seats only moments before the lights went out. The roar of that stadium was unlike anything she had ever heard. It was deafening. The band started to play one of Lochlan's hits and the crowd got even louder. When the floor opened and the platform Lochlan was standing on emerged from underneath the stage, the stadium rumbled. The rumble erupted into a body-shaking, teeth-jarring roar. Once Lochlan had completely emerged from below the stage,

Vanessa realized that her mouth was agape. Vanessa looked over at Spencer.

Spencer smiled and had to talk loudly over the crowd. "I know. It amazes me every time. Never gets old."

Vanessa turned back to the stage and for the next hour and a half was blown away by Lochlan Paige.

Chapter Six

Once Lochlan stepped out of the dressing room shower, she entered the room to find Jamie going over some notes. "Okay, so we have Minnesota next. You'll meet us there on Tuesday, right?"

"Yes," Lochlan said as she was pulling her shirt over her head. Jamie remained quiet. "What?"

"You know I'm worried about the direction this friendship is taking. Please tell me that you know what you're doing."

Lochlan sighed. "To be honest, I have no idea."

"She's waiting just outside the door."

Lochlan smiled before she could stop it. "I cannot wait to see her face."

"Spencer has the envelope that Corbin brought by. Everything is set up."

Lochlan took a deep breath. "I play stadiums every weekend. I don't get nervous, but I've been nervous for two days." Jamie waited a beat before making eye contact. "God, Jamie, just say whatever it is."

"I doubt that I need to tell you that this could ruin your career."

"No, you don't. And it's a little condescending that you think I need to hear that from you."

"If you were in any other genre—" Jamie stopped.

"Well, I'm not, so this is what we have to work with."

"I just don't understand. Why her? Why now? If you know what this could cost you, why are you so this determined to see this through?"

"I just want to be around her. I don't need to make career-changing decisions or lifelong commitments today. All I want to do is spend some time with her—alone."

"That may not be what you intend, but being seen with her could be what sets the ball in motion, Loc. You're about to take her—"

"I know, Jamie."

"You have to be very careful here. Make sure she's worth the risk."

Lochlan hugged her. "I'll be fine. No matter what, I'll be fine. I want you to understand that this could be a good thing."

Jamie sighed. "Lochlan, you're my best friend and you have to know that I want you to be happy. I truly do, but this—"

"I know." Lochlan picked up her bag. "This is my decision to make, Jamie. You need to let me live my life. And speaking of, Vanessa is waiting for me."

"We'll see you Tuesday morning, then."

Lochlan ignored the resignation in Jamie's voice. "See you then."

They stepped out of the dressing room to find Spencer and Vanessa. They fell in line with her and Jamie. They went straight to the SUV that was waiting in the tunnel of the stadium. "Ms. Paige."

"Sly," she replied and stepped inside. She was followed by Vanessa. As Lochlan leaned over Vanessa, she looked at Spencer. "You have what I need?"

"Yes." Spencer handed her the envelope.

"And you handled everything else?"

"I did. When you arrive, everything will be ready."

Lochlan smiled. "Thank you." She looked at Jamie. "I'll see you in a couple of days." Sly closed the door.

"Oh. My. God!" Vanessa said. "That was the most spectacular thing I have ever seen, Loc. You were amazing."

Lochlan blushed. "Thank you. I'm glad that you liked it."

"Liked it? I loved it. The way that you owned that stage." Vanessa started to gesture fanatically. "Like, you made that place your bitch."

Lochlan leaned back and laughed. "I think that is the best review I've ever gotten."

"Like, no, seriously. Do you know how good you are?" Vanessa stopped talking for a moment as if searching for words. Finally, she raised her hands. "That was just fucking unbelievable."

Lochlan laughed. "Well, I'm glad that you liked it."

Vanessa looked out the window. "Hey, that's the hotel."

Lochlan leaned over Vanessa to look out the window as they passed the building. "Um, yep, it is." Then she leaned back.

"Where are we going?"

Lochlan patted Vanessa's knee. "Just sit back. We'll be there shortly. Well, we'll be at one of the places anyway."

"It's not fair that I don't know." Vanessa pouted.

"It's a birthday surprise. You aren't supposed to know."

Vanessa looked at Lochlan for a moment without breaking eye contact. "Is this crazy?"

"Maybe."

"Where did you come from?"

Lochlan smiled. "A library."

Vanessa looked down and noticed that Lochlan's hand was still on her knee. She placed her hand over Lochlan's. She looked up to look Lochlan in the eyes and intertwined their fingers. "Thank you for doing this."

"You're welcome."

Vanessa noticed that she was seeing planes landing close by. "Are we—where are we going?"

Lochlan smiled. "It's your birthday surprise. I'm not going to tell you."

The SUV was suddenly on a smaller runway. They stopped and Sly opened the door. "Ms. Paige, I hope you have a good trip."

"Thanks, Sly." She looked at Vanessa. "You coming?"

Vanessa slid across the seat and stepped out of the vehicle. She looked at the jet just in front of them. Its door was open, and the jet's captain was standing at the top of the stairs. "What is going on?"

Lochlan stepped toward Vanessa. "Just taking a quick trip."

"Loc, my clothes—"

"Are packed and inside. Spencer did a great job at keeping you busy enough that you didn't unpack." She smiled at Vanessa. "Remind me to give her a raise."

Vanessa still looked at the plane. "A quick trip?"

"You'll be home in time for you to be in class Monday morning."

"What are you up to?"

Lochlan was glad when Vanessa followed her without any more questions as they walked to the plane. Once they were seated, the captain came back to them. "Ms. Paige, I am Captain Banks. We'll take off shortly and our ETA is around midnight."

"Thank you." Lochlan looked at Vanessa. "This is my friend Vanessa."

"It's nice to meet you. Sit back and relax. If you ladies need anything, just let the attendant know."

"Thank you," Vanessa said.

The pilot stepped into the cockpit and closed the door. In just a few minutes, they felt the jet starting to move until it accelerated into liftoff. Vanessa looked at Lochlan in the seat next to her. "He said midnight. It's almost eleven thirty now. You really meant it when you said a quick trip."

Lochlan laughed. "It's a three-and-a-half-hour flight. It's eleven thirty now. It will be approximately three when we land, so with the time difference—midnight."

"Where are we going?"

Before she could answer, the pilot spoke. "We're now at cruising altitude. You ladies are free to unbuckle and move about the cabin. It's a great night to fly, and the sky is clear for the remainder of our flight. Approximate ETA at LAX is twelve a.m." Vanessa turned to Lochlan, but the pilot continued. "Like I said, if you need anything, we are here."

Vanessa waited until she heard the speaker click off. "LAX?"

"Yes. A couple of years ago, when I was a celebrity judge on a singing competition, I bought a home just outside of LA."

"And that's where we are going? To your house—in Los Angeles?"

"Yes. There's something I wanted to do with you tomorrow. I hope you don't mind."

"So, this is your second home?"

"It is. I did two years with the show—"

Vanessa laughed. "I know how long you were on the show. Everyone does."

Lochlan smiled. "Well then, during that time I bought this great house, and I love it. I come here a lot to write. When I left the show, I just never could part with it. I always do multiple dates at the Staples Center every year, plus a lot of talk shows are here, so it's just better to keep it."

"I guess I understand wanting to buy when you were

working here." Lochlan looked away for a moment. Vanessa chuckled. "Okay, so what's the deal with the house? The show wasn't the only reason, was it?"

"I was dating someone who lived in LA. Thought it would be easier to spend time with her outside of the public eye."

"She wasn't out either?"

Lochlan laughed. "No, she was out. I don't think there was ever a day that she was in."

"Who is it? Do I know her?"

"I'm pretty sure everyone knows her."

"Oh my God, who is it?" Lochlan didn't answer right away. "Oh, you don't want to say." She could tell Vanessa was trying not to sound hurt. "It's cool. You don't have to tell me."

Lochlan placed her hand on Vanessa's. "No. It's just a habit. I'm so used to not being able to trust people. But I trust you." She laughed. "Hell, she would probably high-five you for getting me to talk about this with anyone."

"Was she the only one?"

"Yeah." Lochlan took a deep breath. "I knew she was an out actress, but we were good friends. I knew that no matter what, Mac would never tell."

"Mac! As in MacKenzie Daveys? Star of the television show *Blue Line*? That Mac?"

Lochlan laughed. "That's the one. I told you you'd know her."

"Let me get this straight. The last girl you tried to impress was MacKenzie Daveys?" Lochlan nodded. "Oh, talk about no pressure."

Lochlan laughed even harder. "Mac and I are still good friends. We just didn't work as a couple."

"How long were you together?"

"Almost a year."

"What happened?" Vanessa noticed Lochlan tense. "You don't have to answer that. Sorry, I shouldn't have asked."

"No, it's okay. Just not one of my best moments." Lochlan took a moment to answer. "Mac is very proud of who she is. She's been on the cover of every gay magazine. She does guest appearances at Prides and on LGBTQ cruise lines. That just couldn't be me. Country music wouldn't have allowed that. Mac wanted me out, and—I didn't." She moved to the couch, needing not to look at Vanessa after that confession. "She was very vocal about the fact that I was forcing her back into the closet. Which, looking back on it, I was."

"And how do you feel now?"

"Vanessa, my feelings haven't changed about my industry. When I first met you, I knew I was taking a chance. When Jamie began worrying, I tried to convince her that maybe country music had changed, but we both know the truth. The only country music artists to have ever come out have paid dearly."

"So, you would choose your career again?" Vanessa's expression indicated her own surprise that she'd asked, but the question was clearly one that needed answering.

"I hope not. I've told myself for years that had I loved Mac enough, I would have done what she needed. I hope there comes a day that when it's someone I truly love, that I'll make the right decision."

"How does Jamie feel about this—about me?" Vanessa sat next to her. "Loc, I get this is new, but you put me on a plane twice this weekend. I think we both know what's happening here, and I need to know what your thoughts are on it. I'm not talking about promises of a future, but I do deserve to know if there's even a chance."

"Ever since I looked up from that app and saw you

standing over me, there has been this pull to you that I can't understand. When Mac ended our relationship after a year, I was sad and hurt, but not enough to change. I've gone directly against Jamie's wishes several times where you're concerned, and that's a first. I can't make you any promises, but that must mean something, right?"

Vanessa's expression turned solemn. "I need you to be honest with me about how you feel. I need for you to tell me if you ever realize that your priorities haven't changed. I'm willing to try this, but I have to know, like Mac, that this is something that, when the time is right, will change."

"I think I can do that."

Vanessa softened. "Okay, enough of all this." She couldn't help but laugh. "But God, you and Mac must've been a beautiful couple."

"We weren't bad."

"I'm guessing that you still aren't going to tell me what's happening tomorrow?"

"Nope. It's my gift to you, and you'll have to wait till tomorrow."

"You're being ridiculous," Vanessa teased her.

"And you are being impatient, Ms. Wallace." Vanessa yawned through her smile. "Why don't we try to grab a couple hours of sleep before we land."

"Sounds like a plan." Vanessa lay back on the couch and Lochlan got a blanket out of one of the bins. She unfolded it and draped it over Vanessa. "Thank you."

"You're welcome." Lochlan settled into the couch across from her.

As Vanessa got comfortable, she looked over at Lochlan. "Thank you for tonight, too. It was an unbelievable thing to experience, and one I won't forget."

Lochlan blushed. "I'm glad that you liked it."

"How could I not? You're a natural at commanding that stage."

"Still not Brinley status?"

"You're getting closer." She followed up with a wink. "I'm totally taking that as a win." Vanessa laughed as Lochlan settled in. She watched Vanessa's eyes fluttering closed. "Good night," Lochlan whispered.

"Good night, superstar," Vanessa answered back just before sleep took over. Lochlan watched her sleep until sleep claimed her as well.

Chapter Seven

Vanessa?" Lochlan whispered as she brushed the hair away from her eyes. "Hey, wake up."

Vanessa opened her eyes. "Hey."

"The pilot is about to land. We need to get back in the seats and buckle up."

"Okay," Vanessa said as Lochlan tried to help her remove the blanket draped over her. She took Vanessa's hand and helped her stand. Once they were moving to the seats, Lochlan's hand still in hers, they sat down and the pilot spoke. "Okay, we're about to make our descent. It's eleven fifty-nine p.m. and a cloudless night here in Los Angeles. The current temp is a nice seventy-one degrees. Thank you for choosing Skyway Airlines, Ms. Paige. We hope you ladies have a nice stay."

The jet started to descend. Vanessa yawned again, and Loc grinned. "Okay, sleepy girl. We'll get my car and head home, where you can return to sleep."

Vanessa smiled through the yawn. "That would be good. It's been a busy day. Breakfast with my family, a flight, time spent at the concert…" She paused for emphasis. "An amazing concert, and now this. Although it has been so much fun, it wears a girl out."

Lochlan smiled with pride. "Well, at least you seem to like it."

"I've had a wonderful time already." Vanessa said just as they felt the jet shake, indicating they had touched down.

"Good."

The captain came over the intercom again. "You are now free to unbuckle the belts. The attendant will open the door shortly. Ms. Paige, your vehicle is being pulled up and will be just beyond the bottom step."

As they made their way down the airstairs, Lochlan's white Range Rover SUV was parked at the base of the stairs. The flight crew pulled their bags to the vehicle and insisted on loading them in the SUV. Within half an hour of leaving the airport, Lochlan pulled into a gated driveway.

They pulled around the circular driveway in front of a house that was very different from what Vanessa imagined she would see in LA. It had five oversized, squared white columns on the large porch of the modest-sized house. In the Carolinas, the house would have gone for a few hundred thousand, but here, overlooking Venice Beach, the price was probably outrageous. Vanessa saw the house with light yellow vinyl siding with black shutters. "This looks like—"

"Home," Lochlan finished.

"It does."

"When I first saw it, it screamed the South. It just makes me feel—home." They entered the house and walked into a completely open floor plan.

Lochlan turned to Vanessa. "This is the part I'm unsure of."

"What?"

"There are two rooms toward the back of the house and a room upstairs that has a living area."

"So, what's the question?" Vanessa asked, although she knew what was coming.

"I don't want you to think that if I show you to a guest room that I don't want you around me, but at the same time, I don't want to assume that you're okay with staying in my room. It's late and I think that we both need some sleep, so either way, that's what I intend for us to do. We have a long day tomorrow."

"Sounds decided to me." Vanessa moved past Lochlan as she rolled her suitcase into the master bedroom. "Let's get some sleep."

"This is going to be a long night."

Lochlan looked over to the clock that read 8:05 a.m. and sighed. She remembered the events of last night. As they were getting ready for bed, Vanessa emerged from the master bath in a white tank top and very, very short night shorts. Lochlan had thought she looked so cute, and as she got closer to the bed, she tried hard not to hyperventilate. When Vanessa climbed into bed, Lochlan felt as though the hyperventilating would likely become an implosion.

During the night, they had found their way toward one another. When Lochlan had awakened this morning, Vanessa's shoulder was touching hers while her foot was snuggled between Lochlan's feet. She didn't want to move, afraid of waking Vanessa. Lochlan had been awake almost an hour, just reveling in their time together.

Vanessa started to move. She stretched and then jumped as if forgetting where she was.

Lochlan placed a reassuring hand on her abdomen. "Hey."

Vanessa opened her eyes. "Hey." She smiled. "I forgot where I was for a minute. Not used to waking up with someone. What time is it?"

Lochlan turned to the clock on the nightstand. "It's eight thirty."

"I can't remember the last time that I slept this long," Vanessa said as she noticed the flashing light on her phone.

"Apparently, you needed the sleep."

"Must have." She saw five missed messages from Chris and four from Mia. "God, they're probably about to send out a search party."

"Who?"

"My brother and Mia."

"Did you tell them where you were?"

"Mia, no. I love her, but I can't trust anyone with this right now."

"And Chris?"

Vanessa didn't know how Lochlan would respond. "I told him that we've been talking. I trust him, Loc. If anyone can keep a secret, it's Chris."

"You speak of him so fondly, and I believe he wouldn't hurt you or break your trust. I trust you."

Vanessa smiled. "I told him I would be with you. He then explained that Mia called, asking him to talk me out of staying with my parents for the weekend. But he thinks I'm with you in Indy." She clicked on the message icon and read his messages.

Hey, sis. Just checking to see how you are
Mia has texted me twice and called once looking for
*   you. Better call her back.*
Okay, Mia is driving me crazy. Where are you?
I am about to send out the special ops after you

If I were with Lochlan, I wouldn't answer either, but to let me know that you're okay would be good.

Vanessa clicked on Mia's name.

If you're coming back tonight, call me.
I thought we could do lunch tomorrow. You in?
Okay, the silent game is getting old. Called Chris. Said you are with your mom. Call me.
All right, bitch, I don't know where you are but it's nearly midnight. Call me.

"Sorry. I need to handle this."

"It's okay." Lochlan started to get out of bed. "I'm gonna make us some breakfast. Whenever you're done…"

"I just need to text them really quick."

Vanessa sent the first one.

Sorry. In the concert until late. Turns out bday weekend isn't in Indy. Text you later.

She then sent the second one.

Just saw your texts. Busy weekend. Can I get back to you Monday?

Vanessa climbed out of bed. "Did someone say something about breakfast?"

Once breakfast was done, Lochlan packed a lunch and they headed to the garage, where Vanessa saw a shiny black Jeep Rubicon. The Jeep had oversized tires, a lift, and black rims. "I love this Jeep."

Lochlan turned and smiled. "That's good, because I have two."

"Two?"

"You are a Southern girl, too. Do you think that I live in the South without one?" Lochlan laughed. "The one at home is almost identical. The only difference is it has four doors and a hardtop." Lochlan placed the bags in the back and lifted into the driver's seat. "You ready?"

Vanessa got into the passenger's seat. "I'm ready."

"Okay, let the birthday present begin."

They spent the day driving the coast, seeing the Hollywood sign, checking out the beach, and doing a bit of Rodeo Drive shopping. Lochlan bought a couple of outfits for the road. She also bought Vanessa an outfit as well. Vanessa protested, but Lochlan insisted she get the outfit that she had fallen in love with at one of the shops.

They returned to Lochlan's house around five that afternoon. They had lowered the top after the shopping, and their hair was windblown from the Jeep. Once they arrived, Lochlan explained that she was going to freshen up and fix her hair. Vanessa did the same knowing that Lochlan knew exactly what the plans were, so she would follow her lead.

It was now pushing six p.m., and they were dressing for an evening out. Lochlan had still been very quiet about what their plans were for what she referred to as "the main gift."

Just before seven that evening, they were ready to go. Vanessa had decided on the jeans that Lochlan had bought her along with a loosely fitting black button-up blouse. She had the shirt in a French tuck and it really did fit her figure perfectly. The dark shirt complemented her hair and eyes.

"All right, I think I'm ready," Vanessa announced as she walked from the bedroom.

"I'm ready when you are." Lochlan looked at Vanessa and beamed. "You look—good."

Vanessa blushed. "Thank you. Since I'm in LA, I hope I fit in."

"Are you kidding me? You fit perfectly."

"Thank you." She took in Lochlan's skinny jeans and royal blue button-down shirt. "You look so relaxed." Vanessa smiled widely. "It's an excellent look on you."

Lochlan smiled. "People compliment me on my looks all the time. From you it feels different somehow. Thank you." She motioned for the door. "Shall we?"

"I'm following you."

Lochlan smiled. "I am glad." She turned to leave the house.

"So, which one this time?"

"Range Rover."

"Oh, we're going classy tonight."

"Still trying to impress the girl," she said as they pulled away from the house.

They had driven for a while when Lochlan pulled over. She took something from the side door and turned to Vanessa. "I'm gonna need for you to put this on." Lochlan handed her a blindfold.

Vanessa laughed, then stopped when Lochlan wasn't laughing with her. "You're serious?"

"Yes." She extended the blindfold farther. "Please."

Vanessa took it and placed it gently over her hair. "This better not be some kinky shit."

She heard Lochlan laughing as she felt the car accelerate again. "Might wanna hold on to that mask, then." Lochlan laughed again as Vanessa's eyebrow rose.

They had been driving just a few more moments when

Vanessa felt the car making several quick turns. She could tell they were going much slower now. "I'm trying to remember all the turns and slow speeds just in case this becomes an episode of *Criminal Minds* and I'm going to need to find my way out of here."

Lochlan laughed and Vanessa felt the car stop. "Okay, you can take it off."

Vanessa slowly removed the blindfold trying to not mess up her hair. She looked around and all she saw was concrete walls and flooring. There were several cars parked about the garage. It resembled the stadium they had been in the night before. "Where are we?"

A man approached and took the keys from Lochlan. "Ms. Paige, it's good to see you again."

She smiled at him. "You too."

"Hope you two have a good night. Should be fun."

"Thank you," she said as she turned to Vanessa. "Follow me."

"Yeah, 'cause where else would I go? I have no idea where we are."

Lochlan ignored her until they were inside the building. They were met by a younger guy. "Lochlan." He smiled.

"Corbin, how are you?" She hugged him. "I really appreciate you and Spencer setting everything up for me."

"No problems. I was glad to help."

She turned to Vanessa. "Corbin, this is my friend Vanessa. Friday was her birthday, so we're here as a gift to her."

He acted excited. "It's nice to meet you, Vanessa. You're going to love this." He motioned for them to follow. "Come with me."

They walked down the hallway until they reached a door that Corbin knocked on. He stuck his head in the door. "Lochlan is here with her friend Vanessa."

He stepped out of the way and motioned for them to step in. Lochlan led and turned to Vanessa just as they entered the room. Vanessa felt her mouth fall open as she looked at the woman now standing in front of her. She vaguely heard the "Happy birthday" that came from Lochlan. She did register the laughter to her side as Lochlan placed a hand on her arm. Her voice was becoming clear now. "Vanessa, this is my friend Brinley. I believe you know her."

Brinley walked toward Vanessa with her hand extended. "Hello, dear. It's so nice to meet you." She took Vanessa's hand in hers. "It's always nice to meet a...friend of Loc's."

"I've known Brinley for years," Lochlan said. "She's one of only a few people who are aware of everything about me."

Brinley smiled. "And when she told me about you being a fan, it was settled that you come to a show."

Vanessa seemed to come back to reality. Her lips parted and she managed to say, "Thank you."

"You're welcome." Brinley looked her over. "Goodness, Loc, she is stunning."

"She is, isn't she?" Lochlan said with pride in her voice.

"No wonder you turned me down for the duet tonight. I'd wanna stay with this one, too."

Vanessa smiled. "Thank you again." Vanessa decided that she needed to speak. Like—words. "My God, I feel so rude not saying much of anything to you. I think I'm still in shock."

They laughed. "Okay, Brinley, we need to find our seats— and let this one breathe." They exchanged kisses to each other's cheeks. "Before we go, we need to do pictures."

"Agreed," Brinley said.

Vanessa got on one side of Brinley and Lochlan was on the other side. The picture was perfect. Vanessa had worried that she would have this stunned look on her face, but luckily, she didn't.

"All right. We'll get outta your hair." They hugged one last time. "I assume you're busy afterward, so we'll catch you another time, but thank you for taking the time to meet her."

Before Vanessa knew what was happening, she walked into the outstretched arms of her idol. "And it was so nice to meet you. Happy birthday."

"Thank—thank you," Vanessa stuttered, aware that this was the third time she'd said those words. "I really appreciate it."

"Don't mention it. Lochlan Paige now owes me one."

Lochlan laughed. "Shoulda known there was a catch."

"Enjoy the show," she said as they left.

They were immediately met by Corbin. "I'll show you to the elevator. Take it to the first level and go over two sections and down to the floor."

"Got it."

They entered the elevator with an attendant on guard. Vanessa didn't speak until they were out of the elevator when she placed a hand on Lochlan's arm, stopping her forward motion. "Yeah?" Lochlan looked at her.

"That was fucking Brinley Wade."

Lochlan laughed. "Welcome back."

"You know Brinley Wade."

Lochlan laughed again. "I do, yes."

"So, we're going to see Brinley's show tonight?"

Lochlan looked around and laughed. "Um, we are in the building, so yeah, I assume we'll see the concert. Gonna be hard to miss from our seats."

"You flew me to LA to see Brinley?"

"I did. It all sorta worked out. She's playing here all weekend and, well, I just fit in. If I had taken you to a concert in some smaller town, I would be mobbed. Here, I'm just another celebrity. There's no telling who is in the seats next to us when we get down there. Here, I just blend in and we can have a good time. So, LA it was."

"You flew me all the way here and took time out of your extremely busy tour schedule to do this for me?"

"It's your birthday."

"Thank you."

"You are very welcome. Believe me, the look on your face, that gasp—" Lochlan laughed. "It was worth everything."

"I did not gasp." Vanessa huffed.

"You did."

"Oh, God." Vanessa's face flushed. "I did gasp, didn't I?"

"I thought you were about to pass out."

Vanessa grimaced. "Did I just make a fool out of myself in front of Brinley?"

"She wouldn't expect anything else from her fans. Y'all truly love her. It's nice."

"Are you just trying to make me feel better?"

Lochlan held her index finger and thumb very close together. "Just a little." Vanessa's shoulders dropped, and she sighed. "Believe me, as an artist, those meetings are fun. You get to make someone's day."

"Or life," Vanessa said.

"Hey," Lochlan whispered. "You slept in Lochlan Paige's bed last night." She stared at Vanessa. "Really? Your *whole* life?"

Vanessa laughed. "Oh, bless it. I am so sorry. Shall I fawn over you now?"

"No. I'll just live in the delusion that I'm like Jerry Maguire. That I had you at hello."

Lochlan started to walk off, but stopped when she heard from behind her, "You did, ya know." Lochlan turned back to her. "There is just something about you. It's not the name, or the status, or the jets. There is just something about you—" Vanessa seemed to be struggling to find the words to say.

"That's all I need to know, then." Lochlan waited a beat as she tried to keep her emotions at bay. God, she just wanted to kiss Vanessa right here, right the hell now. "We better get to our seats. She'll be coming onstage any minute."

They found their seats on the front row to the center of the stage. Lochlan had been right. To Vanessa's left was a star of the biggest movie playing in the theaters. To their right was one of the stars of *Grey's Anatomy*. "I understand now. Someone like you just blends in with the other celebrities here."

"I get to be just a girl still trying to impress you." She understood now that Lochlan truly did blend in here. She got to be a normal girl, who was trying to impress someone she had feelings for. Without judgments or speculations, she got to be the girl who had just made a birthday dream come true.

"You have no idea just how much you've already impressed me."

As the concert went on, they danced with the TV star and took selfies. It was a side that she hoped she saw more. There wasn't a Lochlan that was sexier than a Lochlan who was free to be who she was.

Chapter Eight

Vanessa and Lochlan lay in bed as Vanessa talked at high speed about the concert. "And then she was like—arms up, and then everyone was like—" Vanessa raised her hand and made the gesture. "And she started the song. Oh my God, that was the most awesome thing I have ever seen. And that noise level. Like, only at your concert have I heard that kind of noise." Vanessa stopped and looked over at Lochlan. "Oh my God, people go home from your concert and do this, don't they?"

Lochlan let out a hearty laugh. "Probably. Everyone but you."

As Lochlan laughed harder, Vanessa lifted in the bed and straddled her. "Oh, are you trying to be funny? I think I was in shock after yours." She started tickling Lochlan. "I can't just fangirl over the woman lying in bed beside me."

Lochlan could hardly breathe, she was laughing so hard. "Okay, okay. I give."

Vanessa stopped and quickly took in the situation. Her face just above Lochlan's. Lochlan's toned body between her legs. She brushed the haphazard hair that was touching Lochlan's face. She traced a finger down Lochlan's cheek and her thumb gently brushed across Lochlan's bottom lip. Just then, their eyes locked. Everything that Vanessa was feeling, she saw echoed in the desire in Lochlan's eyes. She slowly leaned forward until she felt her lips touch Lochlan's. Lochlan moaned and Vanessa kissed her thoroughly. Vanessa's tongue slightly grazed Lochlan's lip just before she pulled back. Vanessa paused and looked into Lochlan's eyes. "Thank you so much for this weekend. This has been the best birthday that I have ever had, and it's because of you."

"You're—you're welcome. That statement made it all worth it."

Vanessa smiled a devilish grin. "No, sweetie, I'm about to make it worth it now." Her lips met Lochlan's solidly. She tucked her hand behind Lochlan's head and pulled. Lochlan followed the instructions and sat up. Vanessa was still straddling her lap, their lips never separating, as Lochlan came to a full sitting position. Vanessa's hand brushed the small space of skin below Lochlan's shirt, and she ran her hand up Lochlan's abdomen until she had lifted the shirt over her head. The small amount of time that her lips were away from Lochlan's made her desire them more. Vanessa knew that Lochlan felt the same way as her own shirt was being lifted over her head. Their lips met again the moment the articles of clothing were out of their way.

Lochlan placed a hand on Vanessa's bare back and reached the hook of her bra. With one hand, she released the snap and pulled both straps down Vanessa's arms, discarding the bra on the floor. She plunged her tongue farther into Vanessa's waiting mouth and tugged at the waistband of Vanessa's shorts. She didn't want to force space between them to have Vanessa lift off her lap, so she palmed Vanessa's stomach as she slipped her hand down inside the shorts and under the thin panties that she found. As her fingers made full contact with

Vanessa, she watched her throw her head back, and Lochlan found Vanessa's throat with her mouth.

As she entered Vanessa fully, the hips over her hand started to move in time with her. She wrapped her other arm firmly around Vanessa's waist, holding her while her mouth worked the firm breast in front of her. As she circled Vanessa's nipple with her tongue, there was a moan that came through Vanessa's chest that Lochlan felt against her face. Lochlan could feel the hips speed up slightly and she increased the force of her thrusting and rubbed the spot that Vanessa needed. Vanessa's forehead softly met her own, just before lips kissed her again. During mid-kiss, Vanessa's body stiffened, and her movements slowed, but not before Lochlan was surrounded by the sexiest moan that she had ever heard.

She stopped her movements inside Vanessa as she felt her trying to recover. There was a moment of silence before Lochlan felt the body in her arms shaking. It took Lochlan a moment to figure out it was laughter.

Vanessa pulled her head back and looked at Lochlan. "I was supposed to be showing you how appreciative I was for this weekend. Not the other way around."

"I'll take a raincheck. Seeing you right here is enough."

Vanessa placed two fingers against Lochlan's chest and softly pushed. "No, ma'am." She kept pushing until Lochlan was lying flat again. Vanessa moved her hips slowly against the hand that had yet to move from her center. "As much as I like you there..." Vanessa rose softly off the fingers. "I am gonna need you out for a while, at least..." She slid down her body, pulling at Lochlan's shorts until they were clear of her feet. Lochlan watched as Vanessa's eyes trailed up her body and took in every inch of her, everything about her.

Then Vanessa settled between her legs, kissing her way

up. She covered her calves, her knees, and her thighs in kisses. She kissed Lochlan's stomach just before moving her mouth to her center. As Vanessa's tongue glided through her, Loc grabbed the headboard with one hand while the other grabbed a handful of Vanessa's hair. The farther Vanessa delved, the more forceful Lochlan's hold became on the crown of her head. Loc's hips started to move against Vanessa's face, matching the stokes of her tongue. Just before Lochlan was about to let go, Vanessa took her firmly into her mouth, and with equal and forceful motions, she both sucked and licked Lochlan. That was all it took—Lochlan was gone.

Vanessa slowed the movement until she felt Lochlan's grip on her head loosen. Lochlan moaned a chuckle. "God, I can feel you smiling against me." Vanessa used her mouth again until she heard her name being called out in the darkness. She placed several kisses to Lochlan's core and up her abdomen as she moved along Lochlan's motionless body under her. She kissed both nipples before she licked and sucked along the length of Lochlan's throat. When Vanessa felt Lochlan's breathing return to something resembling normal, she lay beside her, one arm draped across Lochlan's midsection and one leg wrapped between hers.

Lochlan turned to Vanessa "Hi."

Lochlan laughed. "Hi." She leaned over and kissed her. "Do you have any idea how sexy you look right now? Flushed and a look of complete satisfaction on your face?"

"I could say the same for you."

"Who are you?"

"A bookworm, if I remember correctly."

Lochlan's smile fell and she looked from Vanessa's eyes to her lips. She kissed those lips that were bruised and swollen. "Happy birthday, my beautiful bookworm."

❖

Vanessa sat in her eight a.m. class on Tuesday morning. She had arrived in Raleigh just after ten the night before. She and Lochlan had stayed in bed most of the day yesterday after they changed her flight until the last available one to get her home by midnight. She thought of the last kiss that Lochlan had given her as they were leaving the house. Somehow, it was a kiss of both passion and uncertainty. They were entering unchartered waters, and they both realized that the times they could be together would be few and far between. They had gone to the airport together and had separated at the gates. Now she was home in Raleigh and Lochlan was in Minnesota, where she would perform this weekend. They had FaceTimed till just after midnight until Lochlan had insisted she get some sleep for school.

When her class was over, she found Mia waiting outside. She nervously smiled as she remembered there had been a promise to call her yesterday. "Hey."

"Hey? That's all I get is hey?"

"Sorry. I was really busy this weekend and—"

"Yeah, too busy for your friends, apparently." Mia looked away, but Vanessa saw all the hurt that she was feeling.

"I'm really sorry," Vanessa said sincerely.

"We had plans for you. Me, Ty, and our friends were planning to take you out Saturday night. Then we thought maybe Sunday would be better since you were busy at home. Then you said that you would talk to me yesterday, so we planned it again. Now, here I stand in front of your class, on Tuesday, after *I* find *you*, and all you say is I'm sorry?"

"I'm sorry, Mia. It was a dick move and I should have

called you yesterday, but I was really busy." Vanessa wanted to tell her, she needed to talk to someone, but Mia hadn't always been the best to keep secrets. "That's all I have. I was busy all weekend, and I was supposed to be home early yesterday, but it didn't turn out that way."

Mia looked at her with hurt on her face. "When did you stop telling me things?"

"What?"

"I get some vague, half-ass, 'I'm sorry, I was busy' bullshit? Really?"

"Mia—"

"When you're ready to talk to me, let me know."

"Mia—" Vanessa said as Mia was walking away. "Hey, Mia!" It was obvious she wasn't turning around, and Vanessa huffed.

❖

Vanessa had just finished her final class of the semester. She was packing her things and would head home and then tomorrow catch a plane to Nashville to meet Lochlan. There was a fundraiser for the cancer center at Vanderbilt this weekend, and Lochlan had jumped at the chance to attend. Lochlan thought bringing Vanessa to the hospital gathering might help her make some contacts in the area. Several of the alumni from the university were speaking at the event tomorrow. Lochlan and several other stars from the area were donating tickets and signed items to a silent auction. The tickets included sporting events and concerts to help the cause. Lochlan had signed a concert-used acoustic guitar, the hockey team had offered an autographed puck, and the football team a signed helmet. Everyone who was anyone in Nashville would have a hand in the event.

As she loaded the last of her belongs in her car, Vanessa sent a quick text to Mia. They hadn't spoken in weeks, but she wanted to say good-bye.

Hey, I'm heading home. Just wanted to say bye and that I hope you have a wonderful summer.

Before starting her ignition, she sent one last message.

Mia, I miss you.

She read the last five messages to Mia that had gone unanswered. She had tried texts and had called several times without a reply. She had talked to Ty, but he wouldn't give any information on Mia, only saying that the two of them needed to talk this out themselves.

She wondered if she should just tell Mia the truth. It was such a difficult decision to make and one she wouldn't make without Lochlan's permission. It was her career and she should have a say in who Vanessa told. She had told Chris, but he was vastly different. He would keep the secret no matter what, but Mia tended to be looser lipped. For now, it was what it was and she decided that once she saw Lochlan this weekend they would discuss together what would happen with Mia.

Her plane touched down in Nashville at nine p.m., where Spencer met her. She wondered if Spencer suspected what was going on. If she did, she didn't give any indication. "Hey, there, stranger." Spencer smiled as she took Vanessa's bags. "How was the flight?"

"It was good. The hour-and-a-half flights are never bad."

"No, they aren't." Spencer walked out of the airport to an awaiting car just like they had in Indy. Once again, a man stepped out and took her bags, loading them in the trunk and chauffeuring them to a county just outside of Nashville. He stopped at the gated community and was waved through by the gentleman at the gate. Vanessa took in all the large houses. This was definitely not like the attractive, but modest, house in Los Angeles. These houses were mansions.

"The neighborhood was built about ten years ago," Spencer said. "Several artists live within these gates. There are a couple of hockey players, one football player, and two record executives. They all pretty much stay out of each other's way, but they feel safer here gated, I guess."

"I guess." Vanessa was still looking at the houses.

"Ms. Paige is good friends with one of the hockey players' wives. They do a lot of charity stuff together. She's one of the committee members for tomorrow night's benefit."

"Oh, wow."

"Yeah, a lot of local athletes only live here during the season. Some of them go back to wherever they hail from during the off-season. So, it's pretty quiet around Nashville then, but all of the people in this community are year-round residents."

The houses were quite a distance apart to be in such a large neighborhood. There seemed to be a few acres between each of them. Vanessa assumed Spencer was right—safety in numbers. The car pulled into a large home that was covered in mountain stone. It was a beautiful home with neutral colors on the outside and a pebbled driveway.

"Okay, this is where I leave you," Spencer said. The man opened the door and Spencer motioned for Vanessa to step outside. "He will help you with your bags and Ms. Paige will meet you at the front door."

"Thank you, Spencer. It was so nice seeing you again."

"You too. Hope you girls have a wonderful time at the benefit tomorrow night."

"Thank you. I'm sure that we will." After offering a good night, Vanessa closed the door and followed the man to the front porch where Lochlan opened the door just as they approached it.

He smiled. "Good evening, Ms. Paige."

"Harold, it's good to see you as always."

He bid them good night again and returned to the car. Vanessa pulled her bag behind her and followed Lochlan in the door. Just as the door closed, Lochlan grabbed her wrist, stopping her forward motion. The move caused Vanessa to turn, and just as she did, she met Lochlan's lips.

"God, I have missed you," Lochlan murmured.

"Me too," Vanessa responded against her lips.

Pulling back just enough to speak, Lochlan asked, "Flight okay?"

"It was."

"Good." She kissed her again. "You look tired."

"It's been a long day, yeah."

"Well then, let's get you to bed so you can rest."

"I'm sorry."

"Don't be. I know that you finished up with school and took all your things to your parents. You've had a busy day."

"Thanks for understanding." Vanessa smiled in appreciation of understanding her situation.

"I assume you told Chris where you were going, but what do your parents think?"

"They think I'm with my friends this weekend."

"Speaking of Mia and Ty, how are they?"

Vanessa stiffened, causing Lochlan to stop. "Ty is fine. Mia, I don't have a clue. I know I haven't mentioned it, but I haven't spoken to her since I got back from LA."

"What? Why? Why haven't you said anything?"

"She's angry with me that I didn't see her my birthday

weekend, and I can't give her a good enough reason as to why not."

"You didn't tell her?"

"No. I told you that I would protect you, and I am. It's not that I don't want to tell her, but I just don't know if I can. She would never do anything to hurt me, or you, intentionally."

"Do you trust her?"

"You ask me that a lot, but this isn't about me or Mia, it's about you."

"If you think she can keep it quiet until we decide how we want to handle all of this, then I'm okay with it. You told your brother a month ago and everything is fine."

"Chris is different, Loc. That man will take things to his grave. Mia will try, but it doesn't always work out that way."

"And Ty?"

"If Ty knows, Mia will know."

"So, you're keeping this from your best friends?"

"I am."

"For me?"

"Yes."

Lochlan led them to the bedroom. "When you're ready to tell Mia and Ty, you can. We'll deal with the rest, but I don't want to come between you all." They reached the room. "Now, I am gonna need you in that bed."

"That," she kissed Lochlan chastely, "I can do."

Chapter Nine

Lochlan woke the next morning wrapped in Vanessa's arms. She smiled as she looked at Vanessa, who slept with a glow and seemed so peaceful. That ended abruptly with the sound of the doorbell.

"Shit," Lochlan whispered as she tried to untangle from Vanessa without waking her. She walked to the door as she was tying her robe. She didn't need to ask; she knew who was on the other side of that door. When she fully opened the door, Jamie smiled back.

"Morning," Jamie said, extending a fresh latte.

"What are you doing here?"

"Don't seem so excited to see me, Loc. I come bearing lattes."

"Can you come back in half an hour?"

"What?"

"I just need a minute to put some clothes on." *And preferably wash off Vanessa, who I'm wearing from head to toe.*

"Damn it, Loc, I've seen you in a robe before." Jamie raised the two coffees, clearly losing patience.

"Just—I need a second. Okay?"

Jamie looked her in the eyes, realization dawning. "You aren't alone, are you?"

"Hang on." Lochlan closed the door and took a deep breath. She heard Vanessa behind her.

"How's she going to take this?" Vanessa asked.

Lochlan shrugged. "I can only assume, not well." She opened the door and stood back as Jamie walked in.

Jamie looked at Vanessa in her yoga pants, a tank top, and disheveled hair. "Vanessa," Jamie said, the poorly hidden chill to her voice unmistakable.

"Morning, Jamie."

"I didn't know that you would be here." Jamie glanced sharply at Lochlan.

"I finished up the school semester yesterday, so I flew in last night."

"That's nice," Jamie said.

"Jamie—" Lochlan got her attention off Vanessa. "She's going to the benefit tonight."

"Oh, she is, is she?" Jamie's voice held a mixture of anger and confusion.

"She is."

Arms crossed, Jamie asked, "And how did you arrange this? Seeing as I'm the only one who handles these things, I would assume that I would have remembered getting her a ticket."

"I had it handled. I didn't want to bother you with it."

"Bother me with it? Is that what you just said?" Jamie laughed sarcastically. "That you didn't want to bother me?" The laugh from Jamie sent a shiver down Lochlan's spine.

"Jamie—"

"You mean that you had Spencer handle it, right? Spencer, who has essentially become Vanessa's assistant, handled it. Spencer, who doesn't know enough about what's going on to be concerned for your career…" Jamie turned to Vanessa. "Or for you."

"Jamie—" Lochlan tried to interrupt again.

Jamie waved her hand, cutting Loc off as she headed back to the door. "You need to be there at five, Loc. You have press to do and need to arrive alone. I get you think you can handle this, but this is what I do for a living, and you've never doubted me—not for a moment. I wouldn't recommend starting with something of this magnitude. Be there at five—alone, Loc." She looked at Vanessa. "A car will be here for you at six. She needs to handle what she needs to handle first, Vanessa. Make sure that she does."

Vanessa nodded as Jamie left the house. Lochlan walked over to Vanessa. "I'm so sorry about that."

"She's just looking out for you, which I have to appreciate."

"She is, but I just wish that she'd gone about it differently. I keep hoping that she'll come to understand my point of view here."

Vanessa pulled Lochlan to her. "Do we have to talk about Jamie for the rest of the morning? Because I can think of other things we could be doing."

Lochlan was still standing there looking in the direction Jamie had taken. "She knows that I've never put my career in jeopardy like this."

"Right now, it's just me and you, Loc. No fans, no job, and no worrying. It's just me and you. Just two people who want this." Vanessa placed her hand on the side of Lochlan's face. "You will always be safe with me."

Somehow Lochlan knew that was true without any reservations and allowed herself to be brought into Vanessa's kiss. There was a hitch in the pit of Lochlan's stomach as she stepped fully into Vanessa's space and wrapped her arms around her waist. Then fear set in, and her lips just seemed to stop.

"Are you okay?" Vanessa started to step back.

Lochlan grabbed her hand. "Don't pull away." She cleared her throat and couldn't help but be embarrassed by the confession that she was about to make. "I've sold out stadiums and arenas for years. Do you know how many people are screaming out my name? That want to have sex with me? I've never been this drawn to anyone, and I think that's what's scaring Jamie. And me, too, if I'm honest."

"What about Mac?"

"Mac is the only one I've been with other than you. Before her, I didn't trust anyone else with this."

"Wow, so back when you finally did branch out, you really went for the top of the scale." Vanessa laughed.

"You're impressed, aren't you?" Lochlan smiled.

"Over MacKenzie Daveys? Very!"

"Other than Mac, no one ever came along who I trusted. Not with my career."

"But you trust me?" Vanessa smiled.

"Do you remember that night we met? How you seemed to shield me from the people in that café?"

"I would have hated if I had brought you there and those people were all over you."

"See? That. That is why I trust you. Even before I meant anything to you, you protected me. No one has ever done that for me before. Everyone just wants what they can get from me. I have never trusted anyone with what isn't just the Lochlan Paige brand."

"If you trust me with your career, trust me with all of you." She kissed Lochlan soundly. "You're safe with me." She ran her tongue across Lochlan's lips.

Lochlan couldn't help but laugh. "Dear God, you bookworms are hot."

They made love all morning and most of the afternoon. Once it was time for Lochlan to get ready for the event, they forced themselves out of bed. Lochlan wore a gold mermaid style dress. "When are you not stunning?"

"I was just about to ask the same about you. However, you in that little black dress is going to make my night very hard."

"I'm glad that you like it. It's not often I get to wear a cocktail dress."

"I'm not going to make it through this evening."

"We'll manage somehow," Vanessa said, smiling as she moved toward Lochlan. As she reached her, Vanessa wrapped her arms around Lochlan's waist. "We'll get through the next couple of hours, and then we'll come back here, and you are all mine for the next week."

Lochlan kissed her softly. "I love the sound of that." As the doorbell rang, Lochlan pulled away slightly. "That would be for me."

"I will see you shortly." She placed one last soft kiss on her lips, then backed out of her arms. "You'd better go."

Lochlan went toward the door but turned and looked back again as she was walking. "I am not going to make it."

Vanessa laughed. "I have all the faith in the world in you."

Lochlan groaned as the door closed.

❖

After Vanessa arrived at the event, she and Lochlan mingled about the room separately. Even so, every time that she looked across the room, she would most likely find Lochlan looking back at her. They would smile before returning to the conversations they were having. Vanessa talked to several of the doctors and researchers in the oncology department. She met the president of the university as well. Lochlan had been right, it was a night that had given Vanessa even more passion for her desire to help children.

She felt a hand on her shoulder and turned to see an elderly doctor. The look in his eyes was one that she remembered well. She hadn't seen the sorrow in those eyes for many years. Tears filled her eyes. "Yes?"

"I'm Dr. Kadrick."

Vanessa tried to smile and took the hand that was extended. "I recognized you, yes. How are you?"

Her brother's doctor had kept up with her parents through phone calls and emails. He placed his hand over hers. "I'm good. Your parents told me that you were looking to join us one day."

"I would like that, yes."

"You're doing your brother proud."

"Thank you." Vanessa wiped the tear that started to run down her face. "I hope that someday I can have the impact that you had on your patients. I remember you and the way you stayed with us until Mike took his final breath. The way that you have kept in contact with them, and that you honored Mike with a donation to the pediatric unit, has meant so much to me and my family."

"Michael was an amazing child. He didn't allow you to forget him."

"No, he didn't."

"I look forward to working with you someday. If you need anything, please contact me."

"Thank you." Vanessa smiled and looked for a moment around the room to find Lochlan looking at her with a worried expression. She softly smiled to convey that she was fine, and returned her attention to Dr. Kadrick. "I may hold you to that."

"Please do." He smiled at her and placed a hand on her shoulder. "I know that you'll make an excellent doctor."

"I will have the best of mentors. I can only hope that someday I will be standing in front of someone whose life I helped change."

"I believe that you will. I was just heading over to get myself a drink. Would you like anything?"

"No, thank you." She waited a moment. "Could you do something for me?"

"Sure. Anything."

"When you talk to my parents again, would you not tell them that you've seen me?" He looked at her questioningly. "They don't know that I'm here, nor do they know that I'm thinking about leaving NC State early." His puzzled expression turned perceptive. "I'd like for them not to know that just yet."

He smiled. "I'm sure they will be proud of you either way, but I'll keep this secret."

"Thank you."

"Like I said, whenever that day comes that you're ready to make the move, let me know."

"I will." She smiled at him just before he went toward the bar. She took a steadying breath and quickly smiled at Lochlan, who was walking toward her.

"Are you okay?" Lochlan seemed immensely concerned.

"I'm fine." She tried to hide her unease.

"You're crying. That doesn't look fine to me."

"He was Michael's doctor." Her eyes filled again.

"I'm so sorry." Lochlan looked over at the man. "I can't believe that he remembered you."

"He has always kept in touch with Mom and Dad. I knew that they had told him what specialty I was entering. He was just offering his help and telling me that Michael would be proud." Vanessa huffed as she felt her lips quiver.

"God, I wish I could just hug you right now."

Vanessa chuckled. "Me too. That would be really nice. I never dreamed that I'd see him. Never even entered my mind."

Lochlan opened her mouth as if to speak when they heard a familiar voice. "Loc?" Lochlan turned to Jamie. "We need to mingle a bit more before the people feel neglected."

"I just walked over here."

"Loc." Jamie spoke in her "don't fight with me on this" tone. "I've seen at least seven people taking photos of the two of you. Some of these people are your major fans. Hell, they probably know when you last took a shit. You two look like you are having a very serious conversation."

"Because we are." It came out much harsher than Lochlan intended. "Now they can add you to the conversation and the photos." Lochlan breathed deeply. "Vanessa's brother was a patient here when he was seven and lost his battle to cancer. That gentleman who was talking to her was Michael's doctor. I saw that she was upset, and I came to check on her."

Jamie turned to Vanessa with a fleeting look of remorse on her face. "I'm sorry. I didn't realize that this event was so close to you."

"I knew that it would be difficult, but for Mike's doctor to walk up to me after all these years telling me how proud my brother would be—" Vanessa looked away from them. "I just wasn't prepared for that."

"I imagine not." Jamie sighed, and just like that, her business voice returned. "However, that doesn't change the situation here and now."

"Maybe you should go and talk to other people. I'm fine." Vanessa steadied herself and took another breath. "We can talk later."

"I don't want to leave you right now."

"Loc, we can talk later." She smiled. "It may be better for me to have a moment where I don't have to discuss it...or anything else for just a little while."

"Okay." Lochlan gave Jamie a scathing look and walked around her.

As they watched Lochlan walk away and talk to her fans, Jamie's eyes never left Vanessa. "She's a big deal, Vanessa."

"I understand that."

"She can't do this. It will ruin her." For the first time, it became abundantly clear to Vanessa what Jamie wanted. "I'm asking you nicely to walk away from her."

"I don't think this is your call."

Jamie shook her head. "I've seen this before, Vanessa. Lochlan was madly in love with another woman once. But eventually, she had to let her go. She'll be there until you decide that you need more. Once that happens, she'll get scared and realize just exactly what she has to lose, and she'll cut you loose. She's done it before."

"You mean with Mac."

"Mac really cared about her, and the feeling was returned. Mac was much better equipped to handle what will happen to Loc if she decided to go public. She could have helped Loc through the media storm. You don't offer her that, Vanessa. If she walked away from Mac, what do you think she'll do to you? Mac was much more her equal. Mac is an out American sweetheart, and that could have made the blow of their relationship easier. I like you, Vanessa, but you are in *way* over your head here."

Jamie left, leaving Vanessa to replay all that she said. Would Lochlan do that to her? Would she just walk away from her like she had done so easily with Mac? Jamie had been right that MacKenzie could have handled this better than she probably would. God, how had Vanessa started dating someone who made her compare herself to the likes of MacKenzie Daveys? Where had this life come from? After a while, Vanessa decided that she would go to the restroom to freshen up. She had been in there a short time when she heard the door open and felt arms wrap around the waist. She leaned her head back against the shoulder behind her as she felt lips brush the spot just behind her ear. "Loc, you shouldn't."

"I just need to hold you for a minute."

Vanessa seemed to melt into Lochlan, because, God she needed this. "That feels nice."

Lochlan kissed her neck softly, causing Vanessa to hum and turn in her arms. "I cannot wait to get you home with me."

"Me too," she said as Lochlan kissed her quickly. They separated as they heard the first door to the restroom open. When the second one opened, they looked at Jamie.

"Loc—" Jamie glared at them in frustration.

"Damn it, Jamie."

"In case you've somehow forgotten, there is a room full of people on the other side of those two doors," Jamie said sarcastically as she grabbed tissues and handed one to each of them. "Fix your damn lipstick. Both of you."

"I am not a child," Lochlan huffed. "And I don't need you to talk to me like I am."

"You say that, but look at the way you're acting. You're playing Russian roulette with your career. She doesn't know this industry and how they could turn on you. You two can't wait till you get home? For fuck's sake, it's just a couple of hours. Just keep your hands and lips off each other for a couple of hours!"

"I knew she was still upset after seeing her brother's doctor, Jamie," Lochlan growled. "I just wanted to make sure she was okay."

"Making out in a public bathroom is going a bit beyond making sure someone is okay, don't you think? You're playing with fire here, Lochlan."

"If I want to check on her, I will. Do you understand that?" Jamie didn't answer. "You work for *me*."

Jamie looked at Vanessa as if she wanted to say more, but instead, she chose to storm out of the room.

"Sorry about that." Lochlan turned to the mirror and began cleaning up her lipstick. Vanessa watched Lochlan in the mirror as she wiped away the smudged lipstick.

"Maybe she's right."

Lochlan turned and looked at Vanessa. "I know what I want to do, but Jamie has handled things for a long time. I can't deny that there are things she knows very well how to work."

Vanessa thought that what Jamie was working on was her. "I'll do whatever you think is best for the rest of the night. You tell me how you want this to work."

"It's not how I want anything, Vanessa."

"Okay, then you tell me how it has to be."

"Maybe we should do as she asks and just try to get through this night without jumping each other." Lochlan laughed, and Vanessa tried to as well. "Spencer will show you out tonight and have a car service bring you to my house."

"Okay."

Lochlan hugged Vanessa. "Okay, I'll see you at home, then."

Vanessa didn't move as Lochlan left. No matter what anyone told her, Vanessa had just seen for herself how this game worked. Lochlan clearly thought Jamie was right when it came to her career, and even though she had stood her ground and protected Vanessa, she had shut down quickly. It seemed to Vanessa that Lochlan had realized that Jamie was right, and she would choose whatever path would cause the least disturbance in that area of her life, even when it meant following Jamie's orders instead of her heart. She had wondered if she would be different from Mac, but apparently, that wouldn't be the case. Now it was up to Vanessa to decide how she would handle this.

CHAPTER TEN

When Vanessa's car pulled up to Lochlan's house, the driver exited and opened her door. "There you are, ma'am."

"Thank you," Vanessa politely answered. "Have a good evening."

"You too, Ms. Vanessa."

As she came through the door, she noticed that most of the lights were off or dimmed. She thought that she would go up and change her clothes before Lochlan arrived. They had been in the same room, yet so far apart, for the past few hours. Lochlan talked to the industry people and fans, while Vanessa mingled with the university students, alumni, and doctors. She heard a voice from behind her. "Before you go in there," she turned to see Lochlan, "can you follow me?"

The first thing that she noticed was that Lochlan was still dressed. "I can probably do that."

"Good." Lochlan extended her hand and Vanessa took it in hers. She walked with her until they entered a room full of sound equipment. It too was dimly lit, and there were candles placed about the room. Lochlan turned to Vanessa. "Do you have any idea what I have wanted to do all night?"

"No, but if it's anything like what I've wanted, I'm not sure what we're doing in here."

Lochlan laughed softly. "We'll get to that, but what I've wanted all night isn't that." Vanessa tilted her head. "Well, not yet." Lochlan released her hand pressing a few buttons on the soundboard, and suddenly, music surrounded them. Lochlan extended her hand. "Dance with me."

Vanessa smiled and took the offered hand as they found their way to each other. She pressed her body against Lochlan's and they swayed slowly to Ed Sheeran and Tori Kelly. Vanessa placed a kiss on Lochlan's shoulder as she thought about this moment. They had watched people dancing during the night, and Lochlan had said this was all she had thought about. There was so much that Lochlan couldn't seem to do or say in public. It wasn't that she didn't want to, because the way they swayed here in the dark was proof that she wanted her. Vanessa tried to put everything else in the back of her mind, while she just gave in to being in this moment and letting the future work itself out. Right now, she had this amazing woman in her arms, and the real world would have to wait outside that door for tonight.

As the music stopped, Lochlan was kissing her way up Vanessa's neck. "We did my thing, now we get to do yours."

Vanessa chuckled. "To the bedroom?"

"Yes."

They barely parted during the walk, Vanessa's hand roaming over Lochlan's body. Once in the room, Lochlan found the zipper of Vanessa's dress. "As incredibly hot as you look in this, I want it off." Vanessa didn't answer, only allowing the dress to fall to the floor. Lochlan kissed her way down Vanessa's throat and placed her hands firmly on Vanessa's bare breasts.

Vanessa pushed Lochlan toward the bed, and when the back of her knees contacted the mattress, Lochlan sat on the edge of the bed. Vanessa looked down into eyes that were a dark shade of blue and ready.

Vanessa kissed the top of Lochlan's forehead as she felt hands slide across her thighs and around to her ass. Vanessa's hands were on the sides of Lochlan's face, and she positioned it upward, taking her mouth by storm in an assault that caused Lochlan to moan. Vanessa forced her down until she was lying on her back.

Vanessa kissed across Lochlan's jawline, down her throat, and paused between her breasts. She reached behind Lochlan and undid the bra that was now in her way. As she straddled her legs, she took a nipple into her mouth and let her hand slide down Lochlan's ripped abs.

Vanessa stroked her up and down several times as she felt Lochlan's hand moving down between them, and once inside Vanessa's panties, she cupped her, causing a hitch in Vanessa's breath. Lochlan moaned as Vanessa's fingers ran across her entrance and almost gasped as two plunged inside. "Oh God," she whispered into Vanessa's mouth. Vanessa felt Lochlan's hand mirror hers. It didn't take long before Lochlan's entire body tightened. Vanessa slowed her hand and her kisses. She drew back just a touch and placed one soft kiss on Lochlan's lips and lowered her head to touch Lochlan's.

"You are going to kill me."

Vanessa smiled. "That would never be my intent."

"You put those glasses on and become this extremely intelligent woman, then you get in this bed and become a vixen."

"Is that a bad thing?"

"Being here with you will never be a bad thing. I just don't know how much more that I can take tonight." Lochlan laughed.

Vanessa smiled as if challenged. "But, baby, we're just getting started here."

"You don't have to cripple me the first two days you're here."

Vanessa chuckled. "I'll keep that in mind." She slid her fingers out of Lochlan, and with one finger, she hooked Lochlan's underwear and started to pull them downward. Every inch farther she kissed down Lochlan's body, the panties were lowered that amount until they pulled off her feet and Vanessa was kissing the inside of Lochlan's thighs.

As Vanessa kissed her, she propped up on her elbows watching her. She never broke eye contact as she took Lochlan fully in her mouth. Had she not been so turned on by Lochlan watching her, she would have chuckled at the game of who would look away first, before Lochlan's head quickly found the pillow again in complete surrender.

As she worked her body, the magnitude of what Lochlan was offering her resonated with Vanessa. This intimacy was something that Lochlan had been afraid to share with anyone else. Now, she'd chosen to let Vanessa in, and for that alone, she wanted Lochlan to feel how special this moment was to both of them.

Seconds later, she felt a hand tangle in her hair and her face pulled closer. As if on cue, Vanessa took Lochlan Paige to places that she had never been. The giving over of her body was a gift to someone she cared about, and Vanessa valued that.

After Lochlan's body had come down from the second high, she chuckled. "God, I don't think I can again."

"So, you're giving up on me?" Vanessa smiled.

"Oh, my beautiful little nerd, no one said anything about giving up." Lochlan quickly turned Vanessa over, reversing their positions. "It's just my turn to play."

Vanessa cared deeply for Loc and would love to say that it wasn't the thought of megastar Lochlan Paige making her way down her body that was the sexiest thing she had ever seen, but she couldn't lie. She gasped as Lochlan's mouth grabbed her in a sort of desperate assault.

Vanessa's head was fully pressed to the pillow as she let out a moan that caused Lochlan to lock eyes with her, but without stopping her action. As she pushed fingers deeply into Vanessa's pulsing body, Vanessa's ragged voice pushed out, "Oh my God, Loc. Fuck!" She knew Vanessa wouldn't feel the smile that graced her mouth. She was proud. She had done that. She had made Vanessa call out like that. The pleasure was short-lived as she felt Vanessa contract underneath her touch. Felt the pulse against her lips. Suddenly, the smile and pride were gone, replaced by a desire that Lochlan didn't know she possessed. She quickened the rhythm of all that was touching Vanessa until she heard, or rather felt, the rumble of pleasure that came from Vanessa.

Her smile did return when she felt a hand pushing against her forehead. "You have to stop, or I'm afraid for your safety."

Lochlan giggled. "What? I'm just down here hanging out." She felt the hand run softly through her hair.

"What you're doing down there is going to be the death of me, and I can't be held responsible for the repercussions when my legs involuntarily clench together. How will I ever explain to Jamie that your neck is broken because my legs slammed shut?"

Lochlan kissed the legs in question. "And God, they are nice legs."

She felt Vanessa laugh before she heard it. "Please. You breathing on it isn't helping either. Get up here." Vanessa lightly tugged at the hair in her hand, and Lochlan did as she was asked.

"Do you have any idea how beautiful you are when you have your head thrown back moaning my name?"

Vanessa chuckled. "No, I don't. I think I was almost unconscious. I don't know what was happening."

"Well then, maybe I should do it again. I would hate for you not to remember."

Vanessa laughed and stopped Lochlan from making her way down her body again. "I remember. I remember." Lochlan smiled. "You stay up here with me."

"Who's giving up now?"

"Me. Me, I am." Vanessa pulled Lochlan in for another kiss. "For now."

Lochlan moved over to lie beside Vanessa, who snuggled over to her. She wrapped her arms around Vanessa and tried to take in all that had just happened. She didn't have much to go by but was pretty sure that was amazing on anyone's chart. She pulled Vanessa in tighter and after a moment felt the breathing against her chest deepen. Out like a light. Lochlan smiled at what an amazing feeling this was. To be here with someone she trusted, but more importantly, someone she was developing some pretty serious feelings for. She analyzed all of this until she joined Vanessa in sleep.

Vanessa woke early the next morning, and the other side of the bed was cold. She sat up and looked around the room. The clock read 7:15 a.m. "Loc?" Vanessa called out. When she didn't get a response, she stood, pulled on her shorts and a T-shirt, and walked out toward the hall. "Loc?" She looked through the house and into the kitchen, where she smelled fresh coffee. She moved through the house. "Loc?" She made her way toward the back hallway. She saw a light coming from the door that was cracked at the end of the hall. She approached the door and peeked inside. She saw Lochlan in the large sound booth with a keyboard. The intercom was on and Vanessa could hear Lochlan singing.

She played the piano for a moment, then grabbed the pencil that rested on the shelf of the piano and made marks on the music sheets. She started playing again and softly sang words that Vanessa couldn't quite make out. Lochlan had her hair pulled up in a loose bun, and the concentration on her face was mesmerizing. Vanessa leaned against the doorframe and just listened to the melody. She had been there a while when Lochlan looked her way and quickly did a double take before smiling.

She motioned for her to come into the room. "The door is open."

Vanessa came farther into the room and through the booth door. "I didn't mean to bother you."

"You're fine." She patted the seat beside her on the bench. "Come sit down if you want."

Vanessa sat beside Lochlan but turned away from the piano so that she and Lochlan were facing each other. "Good morning."

Lochlan leaned toward her and kissed her lightly. "Good morning."

"That music was beautiful."

Lochlan seemed shy. "Thank you. It's something that I'm working on for the next album."

"I can leave you alone—"

"You will not." Lochlan wrapped her arm around Vanessa's abdomen. "You will stay right here."

"How long have you been up?"

"About two hours. When the mood hits to write, you have to give in to it."

"So your side of the bed will be cold a lot of mornings?"

Lochlan took the teasing as it was intended. "If you aren't up to help me keep it warm, then yes." She placed another kiss on Vanessa's pouting lips. Before long there was a full make-out session happening on Lochlan's piano bench. Lochlan ran a hand down the front of Vanessa's shirt and stopped at the waistband of her shorts. Vanessa wasn't sure if the act was intentional but felt Lochlan's tongue delve into her mouth at the same time as her hand made its way under Vanessa's shorts.

Vanessa's mind was going in a million directions. Lochlan was about to own her right here on this piano bench in the middle of her recording studio. It only took a second longer for Vanessa to not give a damn where they were. She held Lochlan's hand. "Wait." Lochlan did as she was asked. Vanessa, holding Lochlan's hand in place, stood and maneuvered herself until she was straddling the bench. When she was back down on the seat, Lochlan's access to her increased substantially. Lochlan quickly began moving again and returned to kissing Vanessa, who took Lochlan's hair into her hands and cupped her head. She moaned in pleasure and called Lochlan's name.

Breathless and with her forehead against Lochlan's, Vanessa tried to steady her breathing. "Okay, if it leads to this, you can leave the bed early every morning."

Lochlan started to laugh loudly. "Oh my God, I forgot." Vanessa just looked at her in confusion. "My song now has an amazing bridge."

"What?"

"The recorder is still on."

"What?" Vanessa asked in horror.

"I was running the recorder when you sat down."

"Do you mean—" Lochlan stood with a devilish grin

and stepped outside the door. Vanessa could see her through the window. "No. Lochlan, you better not mean that it just recorded—"

Her words died as she heard the moaning that came through the speaker. "Loc! Stop it!" Vanessa blushed as she heard herself groan out Lochlan's name in a husky voice. "I swear, Lochlan!"

Lochlan reentered the room smiling. "Yep, my favorite take ever."

"Delete that, Loc."

"Nope."

"Yes," Vanessa pled.

"I don't know how."

"You're lying."

"Do you know that to be a fact?"

"Yes."

"Well, okay then, maybe it is, but no." She went to Vanessa and kissed her. "When I'm alone and you are back in North Carolina, I may need to hear that voice." She placed a kiss on Vanessa's neck. "God, and it's such a good voice." Lochlan's moan vibrated against her neck.

"What if someone else hears that?"

"They won't. It's my personal system. Rarely do we have writing or recording sessions here. I normally go downtown for that."

She pulled back from Lochlan. "You're seriously going to keep that?"

"I already deleted it."

"You did not!" Vanessa protested.

"Okay, maybe, not."

"You are a pervert."

Lochlan gasped. "Me?" She placed a hand over her heart. "Country music's sweetheart, Lochlan Paige?" She knelt in front of the bench between Vanessa's legs. Lochlan grabbed Vanessa's hip and pulled her to the very edge of the bench. Just before her head dropped to Vanessa's center, she said, "No one would ever believe you."

Vanessa grabbed a handful of hair as her head went back in pleasure. "You turned that off, right?"

Vanessa barely heard the muffled "Maybe" that came from Lochlan.

❖

"That may have been the best spaghetti that I have ever eaten." Vanessa and Lochlan made their way out of the restaurant.

"Everyone here knows that if you want Italian, this is where to go."

Vanessa sensed a pride that Lochlan had for this town. "You really love this place, don't you?"

Lochlan beamed. "I really do. It's not as busy as LA or New York, somewhat quieter than Atlanta. It has this almost Chicago type feel to it."

"I could see that." The more they walked down the street, the closer Lochlan seemed to get to her. Their shoulders were almost touching. "Tell me about her."

"Who?" Lochlan seemed genuinely confused.

"Lochlan Paige. Tell me about her," Vanessa said as if she were asking about an unknown person.

"Well, if you listen to the industry she is a blond-haired, blue-eyed workaholic. She was found on a talent show stage at the age of eighteen and signed a record deal a year later. The following year she had won a Grammy and three Country Music Association awards. She has been a workhorse for those execs ever since."

"And don't forget the legs."

"Oh, yeah, the legs." She stopped and looked at Vanessa in surprise. "Do you know that an insurance company wanted to insure them?"

"Your legs?" Vanessa chuckled.

"Yes, my legs." Lochlan started their walking pace again. "It was the first year that I was named one of the fifty most beautiful people."

"So, the year before you were named sexiest woman alive?" Vanessa continued to tease her.

"I mean, who votes for those things? There is probably some girl in a rural town somewhere that would put everyone on that list to shame."

"What's it like stepping out on that stage?"

"It's a drug. There is no way to explain that feeling. Small venues are nice and personal, but when you step out onto a stage and one hundred thousand people start screaming—it's a high." Lochlan's stared off as if reliving the moment right now. "And when they sing a song back to you—there is nothing in this world like that."

"Your entire face lights up when you talk about performing."

"I have worked so hard to get here. I gave up everything I knew. My friends, my family. I have put my life on hold so that Lochlan Paige gets to fly as high as this business will take her."

"You should be proud of what you have achieved."

"I am. Nothing has been easy. For women, it's different. Three years ago, I sat at an awards show and watched a man receive the highest honor that night when it should have been given to at least three women first. As a woman, you work twice as hard for what men are just handed. Women fawn over them and they rise to the top a lot quicker. Women have to spend countless hours in gyms, eat a third of what a normal body would take in daily, and look perfect at all times."

"I can't imagine having to live that way."

"Yeah, I saw what you just ate."

"Hey." Vanessa bumped Lochlan's shoulder with her own. "I don't have to make lists."

"You would."

Vanessa chuckled. "Of course I would."

"See—" Lochlan stopped walking again. "You are that rural girl who would put us all to shame."

"You're funny."

"I'm serious." Lochlan stepped toward her. "Those eyes. That dark hair." Lochlan's gaze fell to her lips. "Those lips."

"Oh. My. God! It's Lochlan Paige!" Lochlan and Vanessa turned to see three young guys rushing toward them.

Vanessa was close enough to Lochlan to feel her body tense and felt the cool night air as Lochlan pulled away from her quickly. Lochlan's entire demeanor went rigid. "Hi," Lochlan said to the fans as they approached her.

"Oh my God, we can't believe that you are out here."

"My friend and I just had dinner," Lochlan replied.

"Can we get a picture with you?"

"Um—yeah." She glanced at Vanessa and smiled.

One of the guys, probably mid-twenties, handed a camera to Vanessa, almost shoving it at her. "Oh, okay," Vanessa said as they all squeezed in close to Lochlan.

Once the picture was taken, one of the three said, "We are huge fans."

"That's sweet. Thank you," Lochlan offered back.

"Are you headed somewhere? One of the bars?"

"No," Lochlan answered quickly. "We are parked close and were just walking a bit. I was showing my friend some of Main Street."

They all looked over at Vanessa before one of the guys started to talk again. "Well, we are headed to hear some music. You and your friend should join us."

"Thanks for the offer, but we are about head back."

"Come on, two pretty girls like you can't call it a night this early."

"Us pretty girls have to get our beauty rest," Vanessa said before she could stop herself. She noticed that Lochlan almost laughed.

"Again, thanks for the invite, but we are heading back. You boys have fun tonight. Nashville bars can get wild. Pace yourselves."

"You sure we can't convince you to come with us?"

"I'm sure." Lochlan smiled the smile that Vanessa knew she reserved for fans and photoshoots. "We're heading back."

As she nodded toward the car, Vanessa took the cue. "Okay, guys, Ms. Paige has had a busy day. We were just walking off some fantastic food, but she needs to be going. We appreciate your stopping to talk, but Ms. Paige needs to head back now."

"Oh, sorry," one of them said. "We didn't mean to keep her or interrupt your business." He smiled widely. "We were just hoping two pretty ladies would join us for some drinks." Lochlan and Vanessa didn't say anything, which he obviously took as them considering the offer. "You sure we can't convince you? Drinks are on us."

"Like I said, Ms. Paige has had a busy day. She isn't one for drinking anyway, so we really hope you all have a good time, but we will have to decline."

"All right," one of them said.

Vanessa moved toward Lochlan and took her by the elbow. "Ms. Paige, the car is this way." She turned to glance at the three men as she led Lochlan away. "Good night."

As they walked, Vanessa had forgotten that her hand was still on Lochlan's elbow until Lochlan moved her arm and out of her grasp. "Sorry, I forget I was still holding you."

"It's okay."

"What's wrong?"

Lochlan stopped. "What's wrong is that I almost kissed you." Lochlan looked around. "We are in the middle of downtown, and I almost kissed you."

"Loc, they're a couple half-drunk guys that didn't notice."

"I almost kissed you." Lochlan rubbed her face with her hands. "All that stuff. The drug. The me working my ass off to get where I am. All of that—Lochlan Paige wouldn't survive the fallout if I had kissed you."

"You don't know that."

"Do you know who Jamie managed before me?"

"No. How would I know that?"

"Zach Tilian."

"I don't think I know him."

Lochlan chuckled. "Of course you don't. Zach was gay and wasn't as careful as me. Jamie thought, 'Hey, the world is changing. He'll be fine.' He was caught in a nightclub with a guy. He lost everything. He's now bagging groceries at a Trader Joe's on the West Coast. Playing dive bars and birthday parties."

"Okay," Vanessa said flatly.

"Zach never had a chance."

"It's okay, Loc—"

"I want this with you. I want to be able to kiss you. Right here on this fucking street, but I can't." Vanessa saw the tears in Lochlan's eyes. "I have worked my ass off. I missed my parents. The first two months that I was here I cried myself to sleep at night, I missed them so badly. I was in Tulsa when my nephew was born and didn't get to see him until he was three months old. My sister attends college, which Lochlan Paige pays for. I have a road crew and managers and assistants that depend on me to be Lochlan Paige."

"Lochlan, none of that is going to change." Vanessa took a deep breath. "You will always have these reasons to not kiss me in front of everyone on this street."

"Just give me a minute to figure this out."

Vanessa took a small step toward her. "We don't have to figure this out tonight."

"I want to kiss you so bad." A tear ran down Lochlan's face. "But I can't."

"Then we will wait until you can."

CHAPTER ELEVEN

As the plane touched down in Charlotte, Vanessa restarted her phone. She had three texts from Lochlan about missing her already. She sent a text back that emphasized how much she missed her, too. They had spent most of the week inside the confines of Lochlan's home. The warm Southern days left little to do outdoors, but the nights were cooler and seemed to offer more options for activities. Lochlan had been extra careful since the night they were out for dinner. She had made sure to keep her distance from Vanessa when out. Vanessa could feel the tension in Lochlan when anyone would approach them.

Vanessa tried to blame the sparse amount of time that they spent outside on the weather, but she did wonder if Lochlan was in fear of rumors starting. Vanessa was always mindful of their surroundings. She didn't touch Lochlan in public, and they both tried to keep their glances at a minimum and walked a little farther apart. She hated to even admit it to herself, but she could see where Mac had felt forced back into the closet. It was a lot to go from being an out and proud lesbian to feeling guilty while hiding who you were. That was something Vanessa had never had to do. Her parents found out when she was young, but Chris had known first. She had told him when she was eleven. It was while Michael was sick and he had a nurse that Vanessa thought was beautiful. That was when she had known, when she was eleven, and now—well, it was hard to imagine going back into the closet, even for someone as wonderful as Lochlan.

But she had a wonderful time with Lochlan, no matter the circumstance. They had talked a lot about the situation they were in, and their relationships with their friends and families. As Vanessa drove away from the airport, she had one thing on her mind, and it was going to take her back to Raleigh and not home to Charlotte.

❖

Lochlan knocked on the door of the oversized LA home. It was just a moment's wait before she was enveloped in a hug. "How are you?"

"Hey, Mac."

"Well, come in. God forbid someone sees you out there." Lochlan knew it was a joke, but still managed to hit close to home. "When good-looking women come to my house, they are my new girlfriend before morning."

"Yeah, sharing that headline with you is so not what I need right now." Lochlan passed Mac in the doorway.

"I promise not to be offended by that statement."

"I need some advice."

"Okay, you mentioned that on the phone." Mac seemed to be concerned. "Are you okay?"

"Just need some advice from someone that has knowledge of me."

"Anything. What can I help you with? Finally kicking Jamie to the curb?"

Lochlan couldn't help the slight laugh that escaped her. "No, Jamie is keeping her job. This is personal."

Mac stared at Lochlan until Lochlan looked away. "Noooo." Mac grinned.

"What?"

Mac let out something between a chuckle and a whisper. "You met someone." Lochlan shyly looked away. "Oh, and you like her." She returned her gaze to Mac. "Oh, you *really* like her." Mac giggled. "Oh my God, I bet Jamie is shitting her pants right now as we speak."

"This isn't funny, Mac."

"Hell no, it isn't. Well, not this part, but the Jamie shitting herself is a little funny." Mac guided her to the couch. "Tell me all about…" She gestured for Loc to finish her sentence.

"Vanessa."

"Ah, Vanessa. And this… Vanessa, is she in the business?"

"No." Lochlan smiled.

"There's that smile again. You have it bad for this girl." Mac placed a hand on Lochlan's knee. "I don't know this Vanessa, but I like her already."

"She's a med student in Raleigh, North Carolina."

"Okay." She slightly squeezed Lochlan's knee in reassurance. "What is it that you need?"

"I need someone to tell when it's time."

"You wanna come out for this girl?" Lochlan just looked at Mac without a reply. Maybe she was still looking for that answer herself. "Wow, this is more serious than I thought. This is more than serious. You're falling for her, aren't you?"

"That would be crazy, Mac. What do I have to offer her?"

"Um, yourself." Mac looked shocked that she had to even answer the question. "You have you, my friend. You are funny and talented, and you care about people, Loc. You have a heart that only knows good. And you are beautiful. I know beauty, I see it every day, and you are it. You have a lot to offer someone, and none of that includes who Lochlan Paige is. You are taken with this one, and so your real question here is, do you think it's worth risking your career?"

"If that's what I was asking you, what would you say?"

"Do you love her?" Lochlan didn't answer. "Loc, are you in love with this woman?"

"I think I am."

"Well, okay then, that changes everything. If you love her, none of the rest of this matters. So what, your career may suffer for a moment. You're the most captivating voice country music has ever seen. Look at Taylor, she made this huge move to pop and blew up even more than she was. You have the presence, the name, and the voice to do any genre of music or anything in entertainment that you want. You could do music, or television, hell, even films. Have you seen yourself in that short film that you did for your 'Loving You' video? My God, who knew that you could act that well?" Lochlan smiled at the compliment on the video that had won her several awards. "Don't you dare let those people tell you who you can love. It's not fair to either of you."

"I don't know if I'm as strong as you, Mac."

"You are."

"This is what I have spent my entire life perfecting. Lochlan Paige isn't just a country singer, she is everything that I have ever worked for. Look what happened to Zach."

"Zach and Tim got married last year."

"He has the love but lost everything to get it."

"When you truly realize that you love Vanessa, you will see that none of that matters."

"It's always going to matter to me. I only ever wanted to be one thing. A country music singer. What if it happens and I resent her for losing everything?"

"If you love her, you won't." Mac patted her knee. "I

know you love what you do, and you love the people that you support with your fame but, Loc, that one true love is worth it. You know that it is. I know you do."

Lochlan paused for a moment before speaking. "I'm sorry, if I hurt you."

MacKenzie laughed. "No, you don't. Don't you ever apologize to me for that. I understand that it wasn't the right thing for either of us. Now, look at us. You found someone, and I am beyond in love with an amazing woman. I'm happy, and above anything, I want that for you, too. Don't make the same mistakes twice, Loc."

"I don't want to, Mac, but I don't know if I can stop it."

"You can stop it." Lochlan looked away. "If you don't stop this, no one can."

Vanessa took a deep breath as she knocked on the door, and a moment later, Ty opened it. "Hey." He smiled and hugged her.

"Thanks for letting me come by."

"Any time."

Vanessa walked around Ty, allowing him to close the door, and saw Mia's eyes on her. "Thanks for coming. I know that we haven't talked, but I really want to fix this, Mia."

"Okay, I'm having a beer." Ty opened the refrigerator. "You ladies want one?"

"I'll take one, thanks," Vanessa said.

"Yeah, I guess I could use one." Mia finally spoke.

"Three beers coming up," Ty said. His small apartment had the living room and kitchen together, so while he was retrieving beers, Vanessa continued.

"I need to talk to you two." Vanessa sat in the chair across from the couch where Mia was perched. "I need to talk to you because you're my best friends."

Ty handed each of them a beer before sitting down. "Well, we are here." He looked at Mia. "Right, Mia?"

Mia only nodded and took a sip of beer. "Mia," Vanessa said as Mia looked at the bottle in her hand. "Mia, look at me." After a moment, Mia did as she was asked. "You are my best friend, and I know that lately I haven't acted like it, but I need to tell you something—and I need to know that I can trust you."

Mia huffed. "You have always been able to trust me. You're the one who forgot that, not me."

"Sometimes, Mia, you talk when you shouldn't, and I love you even with that flaw, but this can't be one of those times. I know that you want to think I should have trusted you already, but I need to know that you're in my corner here and that anything I say…" She looked at Ty as well. "Is in complete confidence."

"Whatever you need to say," he answered, "we are in your corner, Vanessa. Anything that you say to us, is between us."

Vanessa and Ty looked at Mia. She sighed. "If you think that I would break your trust, then you are wrong. That may be somewhat both of our faults, but I would never do anything that would hurt you. You have to know that."

Vanessa smiled. "And I do. I never thought for a moment that you would do anything intentionally. This is just something big, and it would be hard for anyone." She took a steadying breath. "What I'm about to tell you, though, can't even be drunk party talk. Do you two understand?" They nodded. "The reason that I didn't call you during my birthday weekend was because…" Vanessa stopped and looked at their expectant faces. She decided that she just needed to blurt it out. "Lochlan flew me to Indianapolis where she was performing."

You could have heard a pin drop in the room. Mia and Ty were sitting there, mouths open. "Um, what?" Mia said.

Vanessa almost laughed. "We've been talking since the night that you and I went to the benefit for the Smokeys."

"And you didn't tell me?" Mia didn't sound hurt, mostly just confused.

"I couldn't say anything to you."

"Wait, so you are saying that Lochlan is—"

"Gay?" Vanessa said, and Mia and Ty nodded instantaneously. "Yes."

"I knew it!" Ty yelled and threw his hands in the air in victory.

"Wait," Mia said. "So, she is gay, and she flew you to her concert?"

"She did."

Ty's eyes widened. "Oh my God. Our little Vanessa has bedded Lochlan fucking Paige."

Mia whipped her head toward Vanessa, mouth agape. "Are you...? Have you...?"

Vanessa didn't answer. "After the concert, she flew us to Los Angeles—to her home."

"Oh my God, she is." Ty fell over and laughed, then immediately sat back up. "Is she good? She looks like she would be good."

"God, Ty," Mia blurted out before turning back to Vanessa. "However, those are valid points."

"This isn't about sex."

"Honey, everything is about sex," Ty said, and Mia gave him a high five.

"Anyway, we spent the weekend in LA, where yes, sex

was had." They started to speak, but Vanessa raised her hand. "Let me finish." They sat back and settled in to listen to the story. "She took me shopping and took me to see all the sights in LA. Then that evening she surprised me with an evening out."

When Vanessa waited a moment as she thought about that night, Ty interrupted her thoughts. "Woman! Tell us where she took you."

Vanessa pushed a couple of buttons on her phone, then handed it over to them. "This was her surprise."

As Mia took the phone, they both gasped at the photo of Lochlan, Vanessa, and Brinley. "Shut the fuck up!" Ty spouted. "You met Brinley!"

"I did. She was very nice. She and Lochlan are friends."

"Of course they are." Mia squealed and looked at the phone. "I woulda fucked Lochlan too, after that."

"Right! No wondered you slept with her." Ty kept looking at the picture. "I am the epitome of gay, but I would screw her too if she took me to meet Brinley." He touched the screen and appeared to zoom in. "Damn, Vanessa, Lochlan is really gorgeous."

Vanessa smiled at the compliment and took a minute before she said the rest. "I've been seeing Lochlan since. I have met up with her twice on the road, and I was in Nashville all this week." They both just looked at her like she had grown two extra heads. Tears came to her eyes, "Guys, I am in way over my head here and I don't know what to do. She is very much in the closet and I am not." She began to play with her hands. "I'm over here trying to decide if I want to be the one who ruins Lochlan Paige's otherwise flawless career."

"You aren't just sleeping with her, are you?" Mia asked.

"She had a girlfriend before me who was out. Lochlan

couldn't commit to her when she asked, and Loc watched her walk away. What if she still can't commit to a woman?"

"Maybe she will," Mia added. "Maybe if—"

"I was with her all week, Mia. Lochlan hasn't changed since Mac. You can still see that fear. Hell, you can feel it, as her body seemed to tense anytime someone even looked at us."

"Excuse me." Mia threw her hand in the air as if waiting to be called on. "Did you just say Mac?"

Vanessa felt guilty. "No." She looked at her friends who obviously did not believe her. "God, Mia, I'm doing exactly what I accused you of. Opening my mouth and things just falling out."

"Lochlan Paige was with MacKenzie Daveys?" Mia gasped. "Let me pray to the lesbian gods that is true."

Ty fanned himself. "Lord, the thoughts of that has put impure visions in my otherwise virginal mind."

"Hey, don't think about my girlfriend with Mac."

"Then you should have never told me that that hotness ever existed," Ty said.

"Can we get back on track, please?" Mia said. "You just called her your girlfriend, Vanessa."

Vanessa smiled. "I really like her. But if she watched someone like MacKenzie Daveys walk away, what hope do I have?"

"Apparently, she didn't care about Mac, which doesn't seem to be the case with you."

"Except there were two times this week that I could feel her fear. I could literally see the wheels in her mind spinning and feel her panic. She is that same scared person that let Mac go."

"You can't sit around and wait for that to happen."

"I know, Mia, but I'm already in so deep that I don't know how I would stand it if she pulled back."

"Have you talked to her about this?" Ty asked.

"We did...some. I told her to promise me that if she started to feel that way again, to please just tell me, but then there were these guys that almost saw her kiss me and she totally freaked out."

"No matter what you do, you can't change how she's going to act when the time comes. That is solely up to her."

As much as Vanessa wanted more reassurance from her friends, she knew Ty was right. Loc would have to make these choices, and there wasn't anything more she could do.

Lochlan was awake early, sipping her coffee in a hotel in Phoenix. It had been a peaceful morning so far. She had FaceTimed with Vanessa earlier the day before, but when she kept talking about things that had to be done today, Vanessa told her to focus on her work and call back later. She was about to start a three-month run of West Coast shows that included several guest appearances on different talk shows while she was near LA. She was going over emails when Jamie, who didn't wait for an invitation, came pushing her way into the room.

"Good morning?" Lochlan said.

Jamie took a deep breath as if trying to calm herself. "Who did you tell?"

"What?"

"Don't *what* me, Loc? Did you tell someone?"

"I don't know what you're talking about." Jamie handed Lochlan the tablet she was holding. Lochlan looked at the tweet from an online gossip magazine with the title *Is country music's sweetheart finding love—with a woman?* She looked back at Jamie. "Come on, Jamie, they have linked me to everyone. In today's world, it was bound to be a woman at some point." Lochlan looked back at her laptop again.

"Are you kidding me right now?" Jamie stood next to Lochlan. "We aren't through." Jamie laid the tablet on Lochlan's keyboard and swiped her finger as several tweets came into view that suggested similar things. "They are calling me, Loc." Lochlan took the tablet and looked over the tweets. "Who knows?"

"Jamie, this is crazy. No one has said anything. We've only told a handful of people—people who would never do this." She handed the tablet back. "She spent that week in Nashville nearly a month ago. Maybe someone saw us there." She went back to her laptop and tried like hell to act unaffected. "You know how people are. If they see someone with me, I am dating them. Apparently, that now includes women."

"But Vanessa isn't named, Loc. There are no pictures of her. If someone thought you being seen in Nashville with a woman was a big deal, they would have pictures, but they don't. It seems a lot like someone is protecting *her.*" Jamie's eyes bored into her. "Who knows, Loc?"

"Just Mac. I went to talk to her a few weeks ago about things."

"What kind of things?"

"Just stuff." Lochlan huffed and walked around the room. "My conversation with Mac has nothing to do with this."

"Assuming I believe that, who else have you told?"

Lochlan thought. "Vanessa's brother Chris knows." Jamie threw her head back in frustration. "The extent of what he knows, I'm not sure, but he knows."

"Anyone else?" As Lochlan thought for a beat, Jamie persisted. "This didn't come from your camp, Loc. They're leaving her out of the spotlight for a reason. Someone is deliberately not mentioning her by name. Who else knows?"

"I don't know," Lochlan said in irritation. "That's all I know about. That's all that she's told me."

"Get her on the phone."

"No. I'm not going to let you interrogate my girlfriend over this."

"We have to get a handle on this now. You're about to do fifteen shows in the next few months. We need to know what's happening."

Lochlan groaned. "All right. I'll call her, but not with you here. Just give me a minute with her alone."

"You've got five minutes, Loc, and I will be back," Jamie said as she left the room.

Lochlan took a deep breath and hit the button to video chat with Vanessa on the computer. When Vanessa answered, she smiled at Lochlan. "All done?"

"Not really." She paused. "I need to talk to you about something."

"What?" A look of concern crossed Vanessa's face. "You okay?"

"Have you told anyone—about us I mean? Have you told anyone else recently?"

"I told Chris, you know that."

"Yeah, I know him, but did you tell anyone else?"

"The day I came home from Nashville, I spent the evening with Mia and Ty."

"So, you told them?"

"We talked about this, Loc." Something in Lochlan's tone made Vanessa suddenly defensive.

"We did. You also said that Mia wasn't the best at keeping things to herself."

"You told me that I could tell her."

"So, you did?"

"What's this about?"

"Several of the gossip sites are saying there's a woman that I am, I believe the words some used were, 'cozying up to.'" Lochlan saw just the briefest flash of uncertainty on Vanessa's face. "It doesn't seem to be anyone on my end because they aren't mentioning your name at all. It makes it appear like someone is protecting you in this situation."

"They wouldn't, Loc."

"Chris has known for a long time, Vanessa. Nothing has come from that, so I doubt that it's him. It's been three weeks since you told your friends and suddenly this came out."

"Maybe it was someone you told."

"Like I said, this looks like it came from someone that isn't tied to me. They're not giving your name."

"Have you told anyone?"

Lochlan could see Vanessa was starting to get upset. "Vanessa—"

"No, Loc, who have you told?"

"No one but Jamie and Mac."

"Mac?"

"I talked to Mac, yes."

"Why? To tell her that you're ready to take the big plunge? Or that you've decided you can't do this?" Vanessa spat.

"No." Now Lochlan was angry as well. "I went to see Mac because—"

"You went to see her?" Lochlan obviously didn't answer the question quick enough. "You've been in the Midwest, Loc. You haven't been anywhere near LA." Lochlan remained quiet. "So, you flew all the way to LA to see your ex-girlfriend."

Lochlan snapped at that. "I didn't go and see Mac because of that. I went—"

"Yeah, I'm really curious as to why you would be talking to Mac."

"I just needed to talk to her about us."

"Look, it doesn't matter, does it? You're convinced that Mac didn't tell anyone, that it was my friends."

"Mac could have outed me a million times, Vanessa, but she never has. She has a good relationship now and has no reason to."

"But Mia and Ty do?"

"This is new, Vanessa. *They* are new. Please try to understand where I'm coming from here. It doesn't look good." She watched Vanessa lower her head. "What?" Vanessa shook her head and Lochlan needed to know what was going through her mind. "Just say whatever it is."

"You went to see Mac because you think that you're going to do it again, didn't you?"

Lochlan just stared at the screen.

"You went to ask her if she thought you would repeat what happened with her, didn't you?" Vanessa let out a breath that was laced with pain. "Answer me, Loc."

Lochlan looked at the screen. "I would hope that I'd do better this time."

"But you don't know that, do you?"

"I know that it's different with you. It doesn't feel the same as the situation that Mac and I were in."

"I can see the panic that you're trying like hell to hide all over your face right now."

"Just tell Mia and Ty to be careful. Jamie will fix this on our end."

Vanessa laughed through a tear. "Jamie can't fix this, Loc. She can't make you be okay with who you are. She can't make other people accept the fact that you're gay. You have to be able to shoulder this or you will never live a normal life."

"My life hasn't been normal for nearly nine years. My life will never be normal, no matter who is or isn't in it."

Another tear ran down Vanessa's cheek, and Lochlan looked away again. "You have to figure this out, Lochlan. No one can do it for you. Jamie can't, I can't, and neither can Mac. You have to decide what you want and what is the most important to you."

"I'll do better this time."

"You keep saying that, but I'm not sure, and the truth is, neither are you." Vanessa wiped her eyes and breathed in deeply. "There is dread all over you, Loc. You aren't ready."

"Yes, I am!" Lochlan said angrily.

"You aren't! Look at you!"

"Look, let's just not talk about it anymore. Just tell Mia and Ty to be careful."

"Loc—"

"Vanessa, I'm trying here."

"I know you are. And I know that you're scared. I thought that maybe you could, but when those guys saw us in Nashville, I knew that I would be no different than Mac."

"You are!"

"Maybe we should just take a minute and—"

"No!" Lochlan said firmly. She felt her chin quiver. "No."

"Loc, you have to be ready for this. There's already so much that's happening between us. I feel so much for you, but I can't keep going if this is something that you can't do."

"No!"

"Loc—" Vanessa stopped speaking when there was a knock at Lochlan's door.

"Give me a minute!" Lochlan yelled at the door. She turned back to the computer. "Don't do this."

"Go deal with your stuff, Lochlan."

"I am dealing with you."

"You have fires to put out, and you need to do that, apparently."

"I just need you to tell them—"

"To be careful, yeah, I got it." Vanessa sighed. "This wasn't them, Loc. I stand by Mia and Ty."

"You said once that—"

"I stand by them," Vanessa said firmly. "Go do your stuff, Loc."

Lochlan sniffed back the tears. "I'll call you later. Okay?"

"Loc, you need to deal with whatever you have to. You can call me when that's done."

"Vanessa, please—"

"You need to take care of you and your career right now. If I ever had any doubt about how much you value your career, the fact that you're sitting here about to make the same mistake all over again is proof that you love it. More than anything—or anyone—else."

Lochlan tried her best to steady her breathing and keep her emotions in check. "This isn't like Mac. It's so much more than it ever was with her." Lochlan's tear-filled eyes looked at the screen. "You have to know that you aren't like Mac."

"From where I'm sitting, we look exactly the same."

There was another knock at the door. Lochlan yelled, "Give me a fucking minute!"

"Loc—"

"Please, don't do this."

"I don't want it to seem that I'm making you choose, but you're ruled by Jamie and that life. Until you're ready to say that you're with someone, they'll always control every part of who you are. This isn't about me and your career—it's about you. You need to decide who you want to be, Loc. A megastar who's happy, or a megastar who allows anyone who cares for her to be run out of her life. I could tell how you felt when we went out that night in Nashville. And we both know this isn't the first time. You went to see Mac about your concerns, and I went to talk to my friends about mine. They listened and took in the fact that I had lied to them for months but were gentle in trying to help me figure this out. I will never believe it was them who told."

Lochlan wasn't looking at the screen, only at her lap. She sniffed and wiped more tears that were falling. "Loc, look at me." Lochlan wiped another tear and turned toward the screen. "I can't do this." Lochlan lost it at that point. "You'll never have a happy life if the people around you keep shielding you from being who you are. You can't love someone else if you don't even know how to love you. You have to be willing to embrace that part of you in the light of day, and not just by taking a girl out when it's dark and no one can see you."

Lochlan moved away from the computer so that she was out of view of the camera. She tried not to let the sob escape from her throat, but she failed. Once she felt she could talk to Vanessa without breaking down, she returned and sat down with a thud. "So, you are breaking up with me? Over me asking about your friends?"

"If that makes this easier for you—to be mad at me, and not own what you need to—then yes. It just further proves my point. You aren't ready."

Lochlan then surprised even herself, slamming the laptop closed, ending the video chat. Even in her hurt, Lochlan could see Vanessa's side, and what made her even angrier was she was afraid Vanessa was right.

Chapter Twelve

Vanessa sat at her computer and rubbed her face. "Fucking biochemistry. Fucking cellular and molecular biology. Fuck all y'all!" Vanessa pushed away from the computer.

"Although screaming 'fuck' is one of my most favorite things," Mia said as she walked in the apartment, "it's a little scary hearing it come from you."

"I just can't get any of this. It's like it's taunting me."

"Well, good thing for you, I come bearing gifts." Mia handed her a box from a local bakery Vanessa knew well.

"You got me cupcakes!" She squealed in delight.

"I did." She handed Vanessa a fork. "So how was your weekend?"

"Are you kidding me? Did you not just hear what I said? My classes this semester hate me." Vanessa dipped out another bite of the cupcake goodness.

Mia stared at her cupcake. "You talk to anyone this weekend?"

"Nope," Vanessa said, never looking up. "Same as last week, and the week before that, the two months before that. I haven't talked to Loc in over two months, Mia. And I don't think that's going to change anytime soon." She forked at the dessert. "She made her choice. If I was wrong, I would have heard from her. The fact that I haven't just proves that she's content with the way things went down. I know that I shouldn't have, but I watched some YouTube clips from her last few concerts, and believe me, she is fine. She isn't upset, so why should I be?"

"We don't know how Lochlan is, Vanessa."

"She's off living her life, so I have to live mine, and that doesn't include waiting on a phone call from her."

Mia sighed. "So, football season starts this weekend, I thought we might get some tickets. You in?"

"Yeah. I could use a minute for my brain to decompress while watching a bunch of guys knock the shit out of each other."

"That's my girl." Mia stood to throw away her container. "Jenny and Deb are going too. Game starts at three. We thought we would meet up for some lunch beforehand."

"Yeah, that sounds good."

"Okay, I'll let them know."

"God, I have to get back to this shit," Vanessa said as she moved back toward the computer.

"Sounds exciting." Mia plopped on her bed and stuck the earbuds in her ears.

Vanessa closed her eyes and took a deep breath, trying yet again to run thoughts of Lochlan Paige from her mind.

❖

Lochlan perfectly hit the final note of the song. Just like she did every single time that she performed. "Okay, Lochlan, that sounds good."

She waved to AJ as he was running the sound board. Jamie was at her side before she knew it. "Okay, we have a couple of local stations that want to do interviews with you. Now that sound check is done, we can look over some of the schedules to see if you want to do any of those."

"I just don't feel like doing interviews today, Jamie."

"Did you sleep last night?"

"A little."

Jamie followed Lochlan as she left the stage. "How much is a little?"

"Not enough."

"Lochlan, we need to find something to help you sleep."

"By sleep I assume that you mean forget about Vanessa long enough to shut my eyes?"

"You can't keep doing this." Jamie looked over Lochlan's shoulder. "I'm sorry. I had to."

Lochlan turned to see her mother walking toward them. "Mom, what are you doing here?"

"Can't a mother come and visit her daughter?"

"She can," Lochlan replied. "But when you're coming cross-country, I would think I would know." Lochlan hugged her mom. Maybe a little longer than normal.

"Are you okay?"

"Just a lot going on."

"Wanna talk about it?"

It was then that Lochlan stumbled and Jamie and her mom took hold of each arm. "I'm fine."

Jamie guided her to a nearby chair. "You aren't fine. You are exhausted." Jamie sounded concerned.

Lochlan's mother spoke. "You're pale and you almost just collapsed."

"Mom, I'm fine."

"This isn't up for discussion. These people work for you, I don't. Jamie tells me that you aren't sleeping and only pick at your food."

"Jamie exaggerates things." Lochlan stood and stumbled again.

Her mom looked seriously at Jamie. "Do it."

"Do what?" Lochlan glared between them.

"We're canceling the show tomorrow night and you are—"

"The hell we are!"

"This isn't up for discussion," her mother countered. "You are going home to Nashville to see your doctor."

"I am not."

"Young lady, you will do as I tell you to." Lochlan held her gaze but didn't speak. "I will go to Nashville with you to make sure this is done. Once we have an all clear, you can pick back up next weekend."

"Mom—"

"To these people, and those fans, you are immortal. To me, you are my daughter who is sick. I'm not taking no for an answer."

"I can't believe this," Lochlan said while storming away.

As they sat on a jet flying back to Nashville, Lochlan asked, "Did Jamie say anything else to you?"

"No, she didn't."

"Shocker."

"I was hoping to hear that from you."

Lochlan sighed and couldn't help the tear that ran down her face. "I can't be everything to everybody."

"No one is asking that," her mom replied.

"I can't be this country music star and—"

"And what?"

"I'm never going to be able to love someone."

A look of understanding crossed her mother's face. "Wanna tell me about her?"

Lochlan hadn't seen the moment the dam would break

coming, but it was now. Her crying was uncontrollable as she felt her mother's arms wrap around her and the words of comfort whispered to her. She felt a slight rocking motion as she relaxed into a familiar embrace. It was an embrace from a parent that said the monsters outside the door were kept at bay. The words come out in a sob, "I love her, Mom."

❖

Vanessa stared at the email and read the words three times, but the magnitude of everything they meant hit her all at once.

Congratulations on your acceptance to the Vanderbilt University School of Medicine.

Her first response was excitement and then reality set in. She and Lochlan would be in the same city for the next several years. She already felt as though she couldn't breathe. Lochlan had obviously moved on, and it was time that she did as well. Lochlan would be on tour most of the year, and there would only be a small chance they would bump into each other. But the thought still had her anxiety high. How was she going to live in the same city?

Then the reaction was anger. The first person she wanted to text was Lochlan. She wanted to hear her reaction when she found out that Vanessa had achieved everything she worked for. The hard work and countless hours of studying had paid off. The weekends in libraries and making sure that her dream of being a pediatric oncologist never wavered had earned her an acceptance to the university of her choice. Then the sadness returned.

Vanessa realized in that moment that she and Lochlan weren't that different. They had both had dreams as a child and they had both worked relentlessly to achieve those things. Vanessa had turned down sleepovers with friends during school to make sure that her homework was complete, and she had studied a chapter ahead to prepare for the next week in class. Her entire life had been formed around her desire to be a doctor just as Lochlan's had to be the star that she was. Two sides of the same coin.

Vanessa then wondered the hardest question of them all. "Could I give it all away?"

Chapter Thirteen

Jamie sighed as she sat on the couch beside Lochlan. "Four more weekends."

"Yep." Lochlan read through a magazine. They were on the bus and heading to the last dates of her tour where they would end in cities throughout the state of Texas.

"You sleep any last night?"

"A little." Everyone knew that Lochlan hadn't been sleeping for months now. The makeup artists had been doing everything they could to cover the circles that were ever-present around her eyes.

"The pills still aren't working?"

"They help occasionally. It's weird. Sometimes they knock me out and sometimes it's as if I've taken a Tic Tac."

"Maybe it will take a while for them to help. Just keep taking them like the doctor asked."

"And no drinking. I know." Lochlan flipped the page.

"And since you don't drink, that won't be an issue."

"Yep."

"How much sleep is a little?"

Lochlan didn't look up from the pages. "Stop mothering me, Jamie. I have one of those and she's in Knoxville."

"Yes, tall blond woman. I've met her, and I promised I would make sure you were okay."

"I'm fine," Lochlan said flatly.

"Is there anything special that you need before we get to Houston?"

"Nope. Just the usual." This was becoming the norm between them.

"We need to talk about something."

Lochlan put the magazine down. "What now?"

"Your neighbor Marcus had a niece that was visiting him a couple of months ago. Apparently, her boyfriend is a freelance journalist."

Suddenly, she had Lochlan's complete attention.

"He mentioned to her that a woman was staying at your house that week—"

"Are you fucking kidding me?"

"He shopped the story around to several online sites."

"So, it wasn't Mia or Ty?"

Reluctantly Jamie answered. "No. It wasn't Vanessa's friends."

Lochlan slammed the magazine down. She remembered the moment that Jamie had come in her room that day just after her FaceTime with Vanessa. How she cried uncontrollably and told Jamie to "Just fix it. You don't have to worry about Vanessa anymore." "You and this fucking job cost me the one person who none of you can replace."

"Loc—"

Lochlan stood. "Don't bother me until we get there." She slammed the door to her room.

❖

It was Saturday night and Vanessa and her friends had enjoyed the football game—and a team win. They decided they would head to a lesbian bar just off campus for some dancing and drinks. They had been there for about an hour and were laughing and having a good time. It was the most fun Vanessa had had in months. Jenny had brought her new dormmate with her, who seemed to be all about Vanessa. Anything Vanessa wanted, Stacey got. She had asked Vanessa to dance to several of the songs. They danced the night away and had taken more shots than Vanessa could even remember. That had led them to this moment—in a bar bathroom with Stacey's hand in Vanessa's hair, as she was backed against the wall.

Vanessa felt so many things in that moment. She felt the alcohol, long fingers firmly in her hair, the body that was pushed against hers, and the tongue that skimmed her upper lip. What she didn't feel was, well, anything else. No sparks. No passion. No jolt in the pit of her stomach. Vanessa felt nothing. She pushed Stacey slightly back from her.

"What's wrong?" Stacey asked.

Vanessa looked at the very attractive woman in front of her and realized exactly what the problem was. Being in love with someone who didn't love her back had apparently ruined sex for her.

❖

Lochlan looked up at the ceiling as she lay on top of the bed with one arm under her head. Tonight was the last show of the season. Tomorrow she would fly back to Nashville and begin a long five-month break. She couldn't help but think about where she was this time last year. It was now October, and her tour dates had run a couple of weeks longer than planned. The show that had been canceled due to the snowstorm earlier in St. Louis had been rescheduled to now. Then there had been the moment that scared her entire crew when she had fainted during rehearsals in Denver and was secretly flown back to Nashville. That was the second show that she had to perform before her season was complete. She thought about how this time last year she had walked into a library after the show and walked out a different person.

Lochlan thought of the person she had been with Vanessa. For the first time in years, she had felt free and worthy of someone. Someone who would see her as only Lochlan Westbrook, and not Lochlan Paige. With Vanessa, she could truly be who she was in every sense of the word. She made Lochlan stronger, and with that, she knew she would be brave enough to show the world who she really was beyond the image they saw onstage. That was the kind of person she had always hoped she would be.

A knock at the door stopped her train of thought. Spencer came in. "You ready?"

"Yeah. Thank God. Get me out of this headspace."

Spencer and Lochlan were now side by side on treadmills in the hotel gym. "What are you going to do during your time off?"

"Probably write. Go see my family. What about you?"

"Heading back to Boston to see my dads and spend some much-needed time with them."

"Your dads?" Lochlan was shocked to hear that term.

"Oh, you didn't know?" Lochlan shook her head. "Yep, I am a proud daughter of two gay men."

"That's awesome."

"Thanks. They're great parents. I'm one of the lucky ones. They met and fell in love in high school. Been together ever since."

"Aw, that's sweet."

"Yeah, growing up was a little tough, but every family has their issues, I guess."

"Were kids mean?"

"Nah, parents can be assholes, but kids don't know to be. It was the fear of the unknown for a long time."

"What unknowns?"

"I grew up with dads who were married before it was legal. Had something ever happened to Dad, Pop would have more than likely lost me in some horrible custody battle with my grandparents."

"That must've been hard."

"It was. As a child you shouldn't have to worry about those things. I get so proud when celebrities come out. The more that do, the more it validates families like mine. When you are as loved as someone like MacKenzie Daveys and you come out, people see it differently somehow. They already loved her and knew her. They may live in an area where there aren't a lot of out and proud LGBTQ people and that's something, or someone, they can identify with."

"Yeah, Mac is loved, that's for sure."

"It was people like Mac who helped me come out as well." Lochlan stumbled on the treadmill, and Spencer reached over to grab her arm. "Easy."

"You're gay?"

Spencer chuckled. "I just assumed that you knew." Then a look of panic crossed her face. "Are you okay with that?"

"That's great. Of course I'm okay with that." Lochlan stopped her treadmill and turned to Spencer. "I wish I were as brave as you."

"Why would you want to be as brave as—" Spencer stopped her treadmill as well. "You want to talk about something?"

"How good is your gaydar?"

"Good enough to see someone who is heartbroken and know it." Lochlan didn't say a word. "If you want to talk about anything, you can trust me."

"I'm not as brave as you or Mac. That's all that you need to know."

"Have you talked to her?" Spencer started her treadmill again. "Vanessa, I mean."

"No." Lochlan restarted hers as well.

"I completely shipped y'all." They both laughed.

"Thanks?"

"Have you tried to talk to her?"

"Nope."

"You are a stubborn one, Lochlan Paige."

"Does anyone else know?"

"Not to my knowledge." There was a moment of silence. "What happened?"

"I have a choice to make. The fear of losing everything or losing Vanessa." Spencer remained quiet. "I know that sounds easy, but somehow it isn't. I have worked my entire life for this. I have hundreds of people who depend on me to be Lochlan Paige."

"From where I stand, you haven't been her for a while. Sure, when those lights come up you turn into this bombshell with a bright smile. You go out there and are the entertainer that those people paid to see, but when the lights turn off, you're back to being this shell of who you were a few months ago."

"As long as I go out on that stage, no one seems to care."

"Jamie does, Lochlan."

Lochlan huffed. "She's the reason that Vanessa broke up with me. Jamie wouldn't just let us be long enough for me to make any kind of decision. She was against it from the start."

Spencer stopped her machine again. "But that was your

call though, right?" Lochlan stopped hers again as well. "Jamie didn't lose someone, you did."

"That day was like a tidal wave I couldn't stop. I have been so angry with Jamie since. I feel like I lost Vanessa and my best friend at the same time."

"Well, one of those people is in a room upstairs and the other you have five months of downtime to figure out how you're going to win back."

❖

It was Christmas, and Vanessa was making her way up the sidewalk of her childhood home. She got to see her parents so seldom but loved the feeling of being there.

She knocked on the door briefly as she entered. "Hey, Mom. I'm home!"

Vanessa's mom met her in the room. She opened her arms and said, "Sweetheart," as she took Vanessa in her arms. "It's so good to see you."

"You too, Mom."

"Good. I know it's selfish, but I love knowing my little girl misses me. Even if it's probably just said to make me feel better."

Vanessa hugged her mom tighter than she normally did. "Yeah, but still it's good to be home."

Her mom pulled back and just looked at her. "Are you all right?"

"Yes, Mom." Vanessa smiled.

"School going okay?"

"Yes."

"I know those classes are difficult. I remember when your dad and I were in college. I think I may have seen him half a dozen times during his last three years of school. I don't want you wearing yourself thin, Nessa." Her mother looked her up and down. "Speaking of thin…"

"I started a new workout program and I'm living off coffee and muffins that I grab at the grocery store down the street from school. I've lost about five pounds, so don't worry so much." Vanessa suspected her mom could see all fifteen pounds that she'd actually lost, so she added, "I'm just busy, Mom. It will pass."

"How's school? Grades are doing well?"

"Yes. The classes are getting harder, but it is what it is. I stopped having hopes of easier classes as soon as my first semester in college was done."

"So, school is good, your friends are well, and you don't have time for anything else. Now tell me what's really going on."

Vanessa sighed. "Mom, come on. I told you already. I'm fine."

"You're thin. Tell me why."

"Mom, it's nothing."

"You can tell me anything, Vanessa."

She thought a moment. Maybe it wouldn't be the worst idea to just give her general information. "I met someone."

"Oh, sweetheart, I am so excited."

"Don't be excited just yet."

"And why not?"

"It didn't work out."

"I'm sorry."

Vanessa shook her head. "Just too different, I guess."

"And this explains the weight too?"

"Maybe. I didn't realize I wasn't eating. Over the past few months, I've just been going through the motions. Sleep, school, study, repeat."

"You said a few months. If you've been seeing someone that it's taken months to get over, why haven't we met her? Or heard of her at least?"

"It was a secretive type of thing, Mom. I didn't tell anyone. Hell, Mia and Ty haven't known long."

"Secretive?" Her mom leaned in. "Were you seeing someone who's married?"

"No, Mom."

"Oh my God, is it a man?"

Vanessa laughed. "God, no, Mom. Eww."

"I was about to say…" They laughed together.

"In the end, it was just too much."

"For you or her?"

Vanessa shrugged. "Both, I guess."

❖

Lochlan entered the sound room of her house and sat at her piano. As she started to run her fingers across the keys, she looked over to the empty portion of the bench. She clearly recalled Vanessa sitting there. Her mind played back the feelings of that day Vanessa had been sitting beside her. She recalled the acts that had been done in that very spot. She stood as she sighed. She couldn't believe what had just crossed her mind. She couldn't do that, right? She wouldn't do that.

Seemingly without giving herself permission, Lochlan found herself standing in front of the soundboard. After hitting just a couple of keys, there she was. The sound of Vanessa moaning in pleasure surrounded her. She had been home from the tour for a couple of months, and the silence of this house was deafening. She was alone more—she felt more—and she missed Vanessa more. Everything regarding Vanessa was intensified by the loneliness that she felt. Normally, there were people talking to her, or at her, all the time. Now it was just—quiet.

In December, when the Grammy nominations had come again, there wasn't one part of Lochlan that could find any excitement. The thought that she had put her career above Vanessa played over and over in her mind. She wanted to believe, prayed that one day she would wake up and know that wasn't what she'd done—chosen this over another woman. This felt different from Mac. This time it was Vanessa, and everything about the breakup left a much viler taste in her mouth.

She turned off the sounds of Vanessa and walked through the house. She passed a minibar and stopped just in front of it. Lochlan had never been a drinker. She had a glass of wine occasionally at functions, but it never extended any further. But the sadness that she felt made this moment seem like a good place to start. She grabbed one of the bottles and walked back to the sound room. She returned to her seat and put the bottle on the piano shelf. She played for a while, contemplating what to do. She played and played until she stopped and looked at the bottle before her.

She removed the bottle cap and took a sip. She pulled the bottle back and looked at the black label. "Good God, why do people drink that shit?" But a moment later, she returned it to her lips and turned the bottle up. After a long drink, she could feel the sting of the alcohol in her throat and chest. She returned the bottle to the top of the piano. She played again as the liquid took its effect. She picked up the pencil on the piano and started to jot down lyrics. She took another sip and returned the bottle to its place. She played a melody to the words she had written.

Hours later, Lochlan decided that she needed to put

everything down. She went to the kitchen to get her medication to help her sleep, but she thought of more lyrics. She returned to the sound room and sat down. She wrote some more and took another drink. She looked at the bottle of liquor and saw the medication bottle to its right. "Did I take those?" She tried to clear her foggy memory. No, she hadn't. She was almost sure of it. She took a pill and downed it with the bottle of liquid that now seemed to burn a little less. She played the piano again and wrote down the lyrics that she thought would go perfectly.

She took her phone off the piano and called Spencer. "Hey."

"Lochlan? Are you okay? Your voice sounds a little… slurred."

"I'm fine." She grabbed the sheet music off the desk and shook it in excitement. "You should hear this song, Spencer."

"Lochlan, how much have you had to drink?"

"Not much." She placed her phone on speaker and set it on the bench beside her. "Just listen." The song was about a woman who had a broken heart at her own hands but was trying to find the strength to make things right again.

"Lochlan, that's beautiful." Spencer chuckled. "Only Lochlan Paige could do that flawlessly and intoxicated at the same time."

"It's Vanessa's song," Lochlan said sadly.

"I'm sure that she'll love it."

"I need to play it for her."

"How about tomorrow?" Spencer said. "It's nearly midnight, so it's after one there. It's a beautiful song, but maybe you need to get some sleep."

"Yeah, maybe." She looked at the piano again. "I better take my medication to help me sleep." Lochlan paused. "I can't sleep without her, Spencer. I haven't really slept in months."

"I know, Loc."

"I miss her. I miss her really bad."

"Just take the meds if you need to and try to get some sleep. You'll feel better in the morning. Drink a glass of water before bed, and I'll check on you in the morning."

Lochlan turned the bottle up, washing the medication down. "Okay. I'll try and sleep."

"Good. Drink the water, Lochlan."

"I will." She pulled the music sheet closer so that her suddenly blurry eyes could see. "I'm just going to work a little longer."

"You need to sleep."

"I will," Lochlan replied.

"And no calling Vanessa tonight. Okay?"

"Okay. I'll call her tomorrow."

"I'm sure she would love to hear from you."

"I'm gonna tell her that I love her."

"I am happy for you. For now, go to sleep, so tomorrow when you play her the song, and tell her you love her, it will be with a clear head."

"Okay. I'll wait."

"Good girl."

"I need to finish this, then go to bed. 'Night."

"'Night, Loc." Spencer laughed.

After hanging up the phone, Lochlan continued to write for another half an hour. She tried to stand and make her way to the bedroom. She looked at the nearly empty bottle of liquor, thinking she would just finish it off. As she did, she realized she needed to take her medication. She was proud of the songs she'd written tonight. There were six she'd written and thought that maybe four or five would be chart toppers. Lochlan didn't really understand why people enjoyed drinking. She rarely did. She didn't like the feel of the room spinning or the way her face felt numb. As she took a step away from the piano, the room around her started to tilt severely. She grabbed hold of the edge of the piano just before everything went dark, and she felt herself falling.

CHAPTER FOURTEEN

Good morning," the anchor said during the nationally televised morning show. "We have some breaking news out of Nashville. Country music star Lochlan Paige was found unresponsive this morning by one of her assistants. The star was taken to a local hospital, where her condition is unknown. Sources on the scene have said that EMTs were fiercely working on Paige as they departed the Davidson County home. All requests for comments or further information are not being returned at this time."

Vanessa stood with tears streaming down her face while Mia and Ty tried to console her. Her voice was raspy from the crying that she had apparently been doing for quite a while. "I can't...I saw it on Twitter almost an hour ago. It's all over the radio." She held her phone out. "Jamie isn't answering her calls, and no one is answering Lochlan's phone. I don't know what's going on."

Mia took her in her arms and pulled her into the room. "We'll get someone on the phone, okay?"

"I'm studying to be a doctor and know enough about the human body to know what happens when they find people unresponsive, and how they got that way. And what happens to their brains when they're down too long." Mia rubbed one shoulder while Ty rubbed the other. "She wouldn't do that, right?"

"Honey, we don't know," Ty said sympathetically. "We just don't know yet."

Vanessa pulled away from them. "I need to talk to Jamie." Vanessa dialed again. "Damn it! Why isn't she answering her damn phone?"

A voice came back over the television. They turned to the screen as the anchor continued. "We have some new details on the Lochlan Paige story." They froze. "We're hearing reports that Lochlan is now in critical but stable condition. We also have reports saying that open bottles of liquor and sleeping pills were found at the scene. We have no confirmation on this as of now, but from what we understand, her use of sleeping pills was known by several in her inner circle. We have the tip from a very reliable source here at the residence, and any allegations have yet to be confirmed or denied by Lochlan's team."

"Turn it off!" Vanessa screamed as the anchor continued to talk. Mia and Ty just stared at her as if not knowing what to do. "Turn it. The fuck. Off!"

Ty jumped toward the television that was now showing scenes from Lochlan's Nashville home as emergency vehicles drove away. "They said it was unconfirmed, Vanessa. It's probably someone trying to make a name for themselves."

"Do you really believe that? She's a superstar living a lie." Neither said anything. "Do you really think it's not true?"

Mia was the first to speak. "You know her better than we do. You tell us."

❖

Vanessa heard the phone ring in the living room and Mia quickly answered it. She went back to the room as Mia said, "Hold on, I will get her."

Vanessa quickly took the phone. "Hello."

"It's Jamie."

Vanessa lost her breath. "What happened? How is she? What the hell happened, Jamie?"

"You know what I do, Vanessa. Spencer talked to her last night and she was writing. We think that she was confused as to whether she had taken her sleeping pills because she was drinking."

"Drinking?"

"You're as surprised as I am." Jamie sighed. "Spencer wasn't aware that Lochlan can't drink with the new medications that she is on. No one told her that because there was no reason to know—well, we thought there was no reason. Spencer went to the house this morning and found her."

"What kind of medication?"

"It's a sleep medication." There was a pause before Jamie spoke again. "She hasn't been sleeping well."

"For how long?"

Again, there was silence for a moment. "Since the breakup."

"I thought she was okay," Vanessa said softly as she sat down. "I thought she was okay," she repeated.

"I'm at her house trying to clean up the mess the EMTs made before her parents have to see this. She was upgraded to stable condition about an hour ago. They pumped her stomach upon arrival."

Again, there was silence.

"I'm sorry that I haven't called you. I don't have your contact information and wasn't able to get it until I was here at

Lochlan's. I didn't even know if you wanted that. I just found her phone and saw your calls, so—"

"What's this going to mean for her?"

"I believe it was an accident, and Spencer knows she was confused about the meds, so I don't know if any kind of outpatient care will be asked for by her doctors or the powers that be. But the media will hound her until she gives up the reason why it happened." Jamie sighed. "You may want to prepare yourself for that possibility. Lochlan's staff will try to make sure that you're protected, but it may lead back to you."

"I'm fine with all that, Jamie. I just want her to be okay."

"She will be. In time. She woke up just before I left but was too medicated to talk. She was still pretty groggy and fell right back to sleep."

"I hate that this is forcing her hand."

Jamie chuckled. "It didn't force much. Lochlan has been a ticking time bomb lately."

"What do you mean?"

"Well, she was working on the next album. I would say that ninety percent of the tracks were about you."

"They were?"

"Spencer said that she sang her one last night, and if these song sheets in my hands are any indication, then yes." Jamie sighed. "She wasn't going to stay away from you much longer, Vanessa. She also wasn't staying in that closet, and whether or not it caused this, I assume it just put that decision on a fast track."

"I love her, Jamie. I want you to understand that. She isn't doing this for someone who isn't in this for the long haul. I love her."

"I know that you do," Jamie answered. "This is my fault."

"Jamie—"

"It's true, and we both know it. I pushed her too hard. I did what I thought was best for her career at any cost to her." Jamie sarcastically laughed. "I am a horrible friend."

"No, you aren't." Vanessa even surprised herself. "You did what you thought was best for her. I didn't agree with it, but I know it wasn't out of malice."

"I need to head back to the hospital. I just came to clean up a bit before they got here. I'll have Loc's phone with me, so I have your number." After another few seconds, she said, "She would want you here. She would want for us to make sure that you were okay—and not alone."

"Are you sure about that?"

"She would want you here."

"I can pack a bag and be there in the morning." Vanessa stood to retrieve her luggage.

"Can I call you right back?"

"Um, sure."

"Is anyone with you? You may not want to travel alone."

"My best friends Ty and Mia are here now." Vanessa turned to them. "Maybe I can talk them into riding down with me." They both nodded. "Yeah, they're coming with me."

"Okay, let me call you right back."

In ten minutes, Jamie was on the phone again giving Vanessa instructions on a flight. She had booked a jet, and it would be waiting when they arrived at the airport. Jamie told her that she would meet her when she landed in Nashville and would take her to Lochlan.

"Thank you, Jamie."

"Don't thank me. I feel like I've been protecting a lot of things lately, but now I'm just not sure that any of them were Lochan." Jamie sniffed. "She would want you here with us. You deserve to be here."

"Thank you."

"We both care about her and we have to make sure that she's okay." Vanessa wasn't even sure if Jamie was speaking to her or just talking out loud.

"We will, Jamie. Lochlan wasn't ready for what coming out would cost her, so this doesn't all fall on you."

Jamie sighed. "I wish I believed you."

❖

Vanessa, Mia, and Ty touched down in Nashville and were met by Jamie and Spencer. Vanessa walked into Spencer's open arms.

I am so glad that you're here."

Vanessa nodded against her shoulder, as fresh tears rolled down her cheeks. "I wouldn't be anywhere else."

On the way to the hospital, Jamie explained to Vanessa what was going on with Lochlan's record label. "The record label was trying to step in."

"And do what?"

"Their take on the situation was that Lochlan, a woman who never drank, needed help," Jamie said in frustration.

"That's crazy."

"I went to bat for her, but the label said that it would send a good message to the fans that were dealing with similar issues to see her accept what had happened."

"Do you think that will stand?"

"They don't know her, Vanessa. I can say she doesn't have a problem, and you can say that, but they are looking at this from the outside. They're covering their own asses."

"What are we talking?"

"If they get their way?" Vanessa nodded. "Thirty days rehab. Once released from the hospital, Lochlan will be transferred to a treatment center in Los Angeles."

"Surely you can fight this?"

"The media outlets are running two very different stories. Half are saying that Lochlan was a drug-addicted star who had been battling depression. The other half seem to think she was a star that was exhausted after years of appearances and concert dates. The powers that be have to look proactive no matter what it seems to say about Loc."

Vanessa was silent for a moment. "What about Mac's tweet? Even she said that everyone close to Lochlan knows that she doesn't drink. Not to mention, four different bands who toured with her have said the same thing."

"She is definitely the hot topic today amongst talk shows. They're questioning if we missed something." Jamie looked away. "We know why this happened. They don't." There was a pause. "Not yet anyway."

When Vanessa arrived, she was introduced to Lochlan's family and was given a moment alone with Lochlan. Once everyone was out of the room, she took the still, pale hand in hers. "I'm here, Loc. Everything is going to be okay. We just need for you to wake up." She kissed her on the cheek. "And I'll be right here when you do."

A short time later, the door opened and Lochlan's sister entered the room. Kayla handed a coffee to Vanessa. "My sister tells me that you're hardcore and drink coffee at night."

Vanessa smiled at the memory of her and Lochlan the first night they met. "Thank you."

"You're welcome."

"So, you knew?"

"She told us, yeah." Kayla sat in the chair on the other side of Lochlan's bed. "When she almost collapsed that night—"

"When she what?" Vanessa asked.

"It was sometime in September. It was kept very quiet from the media. Mom was up visiting her and said that Lochlan just seemed drained. They took her to Nashville and she had to follow up with her doctor, who said that Loc wasn't sleeping. That's when the sleeping pills were prescribed. She told me about you." Kayla laughed. "I mean, she told me all about you. The girl talked for hours."

"Her whole life has had to be a damned secret," Vanessa said.

"It does, and it sucks. She's always protecting someone. She's always made sure that we were all okay. Brad and Kyle had college paid for thanks to Loc. Casey, our nephew, has a trust fund already in place that is bigger than most people's lifetime wages. With money from her second album, she bought Mom and Dad a new house. I got a full ride at the University of Tennessee, but she makes sure that everything I need or want is covered. She's always taken care of us." Kayla sighed. "Sometimes I think my bullheaded sister thinks that if anything ever happened to her, we would all fall apart. She worries about us and Jamie and Eli. She worries about every assistant and every band member. She thinks if Lochlan Paige is out of a job, so is everyone else." Kayla looked at Vanessa. "My sister didn't do this on purpose, Vanessa. I know her. She's just under too much stress right now, and because of that, she couldn't sleep. Jamie said sometimes the pills worked, others they didn't. It depended on her stress level. She said there were nights Lochlan took those damn things and didn't sleep for hours afterward. We believe that's the reason she forgot she had taken them, they weren't kicking in."

Vanessa sighed. "I don't know what to do to help her."

"I know that you don't. We all get it. Mac called me earlier." Vanessa looked at her knowingly. "By that look, I assume that you know about them." Vanessa nodded. "She's freaking out."

"I'm sure." Even Vanessa could hear the jealousy in her voice.

Kayla chuckled. "It's not like that. Mac is totally and completely in love with someone else. She and Loc have been friends for years, good friends, and probably always will be. Loc has been talking to Mac a lot lately. She's of the belief that Loc was about to come out on her own."

"Jamie seem to think the same thing?"

"Yeah, apparently." Kayla smiled. "She told Mac last week that she couldn't do this anymore." A tear ran down Vanessa's cheek. "Mac said that Loc's entire next album was going to be songs that she wrote about you. Mac said that she had never been so proud of Loc. Said that she had finally found someone who was worth all the risks."

"God, Loc."

Kayla couldn't help but laugh. "Oh, and she told me about Brinley." Vanessa started to laugh too. "She also told Mac. I remember her saying," Kayla straightened and did her best Lochlan impression, "'She doesn't get that starstruck over me.'"

They laughed. "I just never let it show." Vanessa's eyes widened. "Do you know how good Loc is in concert?"

"Yep," Kayla said proudly. "Seen her several times. Amazed every single time."

The door opened and a few nurses walked in. They checked Lochlan's vitals and charted her bloodwork.

One of the nurses smiled. "I'm a huge fan of hers. Not really supposed to tell you that, but there it is."

"Thank you," Kayla replied.

"We're all hoping she wakes soon. Everything looks good and we don't think it'll be much longer." The nurse looked over at Lochlan. "She's just catching up on some sleep." She motioned to the two couches in the room. "Those turn into a bed, and I'll bring in some pillows and blankets for you. It's getting late and I'm sure that you all need some sleep."

"I think most of us are going to Loc's for the night." Kayla looked at Vanessa. "A couple of us will stay, but the majority are heading out shortly."

"Well, there's plenty of room. I can wheel in an extra recliner if we need it," the nurse said.

"The one that we have should be plenty," Vanessa said.

Lochlan's parents and brothers came back in the room. "Okay, kids," Lochlan's mom said. "We need to leave Loc alone and let her rest." She turned to Brad and Kyle. "You boys go with your dad." She turned to Kayla.

"Nope, I'm staying right here," Kayla answered before her mom could say a word.

"Figured as much." She smiled and turned to Vanessa. "Honey, what would you like to do?"

"Can I stay?"

Lochlan's dad spoke up. "Do you have any idea the hell we'd catch from that one," he motioned to Lochlan, "if we even thought of making you leave?"

Vanessa smiled. "Okay, then, I would like to stay."

They turned to look at Mia and Ty. "What about you two?" Kayla said. "You can stay with Vanessa or head over to Loc's with Dad. Totally up to you."

Vanessa caught the looks in their eyes. "I'm fine, guys. If you want to stay, you can, but you may need to get some rest. You can go with them and come back in the morning."

"Are you sure?" Ty asked.

"I am. No need for everyone to be exhausted on the first day."

"So, I guess that we'll head to the house with them." Mia went over to hug Vanessa.

Ty hugged her as well. "If you can't sleep, call. I'll put Mia on the phone and she can bore you to sleep."

"Thanks. I'll keep that in mind."

Lochlan's dad and bothers hugged Vanessa. "We're a hugging family," Brad said to Vanessa. "I think you better get used to that."

She loved the fact that Lochlan came from a family just as close as her own. Once everyone was gone, Kayla found a spot on the couch across the room, leaving the couch to Lochlan's mom. They had pulled one of the recliners over to Lochlan's bed where Vanessa snuggled in. She lay on her left side and raised her right hand out from under the blanket, placing it firmly on Lochlan's.

The lights in the room were turned down and the rhythmic sounds of the monitors lulled them to sleep.

Chapter Fifteen

Lochlan took a deep breath before opening her eyes. She could hear unfamiliar noises around her. She heard the faint voices of people talking from a distance. Maybe outside her hotel room door? Why did people always have to be so loud in hotel hallways? She'd never understood that. And what the hell was that beeping? She slightly opened her eyes and looked to the left side of the room. She blinked several times until the figures came into view. *Mom? Kayla? Where am I?*

It was then that she turned to the right of her bed and found a sleeping form snuggled under a blanket. Her gaze fell on the relaxed features of Vanessa's face. *She looks uncomfortable.* Lochlan tried to move her hand, attempting to find the top of Vanessa's head as she slept. She gently brushed over the hair. "Vanessa," Lochlan groaned.

At that, three heads in the room shot up. Lochlan groaned again at the sudden movement of her hand that was on Vanessa's head.

"Loc." Vanessa seemed very excited to see her. "Hey," she said softly.

"Where the hell am I?"

Her mom looked down at her. "You're in the hospital, sweetie."

"What? Why? What happened?" She grimaced. "And why is my shoulder killing me?"

"You fell," Vanessa answered. "They said there's some bruising, but nothing is broken."

"Well, that's good, I guess."

"Yes," Vanessa said, "that is very good. We frown on broken bones." She smiled.

Just then the reality of the situation hit. "You're here?" She looked at Vanessa wearily. "Why?"

Vanessa glanced at Lochlan's mom. "I can leave if—"

"No!" Lochlan said and grabbed her hand. "No. You and my mom, who don't know each other, are in this room together. What happened to me that would make them call you?"

Before anyone could answer, Kayla and three nurses entered the room. "Hello, Ms. Westbrook."

"Hi," Lochlan replied nervously.

"The doctor is on her way in. We're gonna get some vitals really quick before she gets here."

Lochlan nodded as Kayla spoke. "I just texted Dad. He's having coffee with Jamie, so she knows the update."

"Will someone please tell me what the hell happened?"

Before anyone could answer, a doctor entered the room. "Ms. Westbrook. How are you?"

"Very confused," Lochlan answered.

The doctor examined Lochlan's pupils. "What kind of confused? Are you having memory issues? There was a small bump to the head—"

"Well, that would explain the headache."

"We'll get you something for that," the doctor said as she continued to examine Lochlan.

"I just want to know what happened."

"What was the last thing you remember?" the doctor asked.

"I was—" Lochlan thought hard. "I was at home—writing and working on music."

"What else?"

Lochlan closed her eyes. "That damned tequila. God." She could almost still taste it. "I don't ever drink, but for some reason—" She stopped and thought of the exact reason. She wouldn't say it out loud. Not with Vanessa in the room.

"We know that you were writing…" Kayla looked toward Lochlan. "And we thought that may have been why you needed a drink. Like, maybe it wasn't going well. I mean, since you don't even drink, we thought—"

Lochlan stopped her rambling sister. "I drank some tequila and went back to writing. It got late, so I left the room and took my medicine."

"Your sleeping medication?" the doctor asked.

"Yeah," Lochlan said. "I usually only take vitamins, but yes, I've been taking sleeping medication lately."

"Did they tell you not to mix the medication with alcohol?"

"Oh my God. They did—well, Jamie did. I don't usually drink, so it didn't cross my mind."

"But you did drink that night?"

Lochlan looked down, ashamed. "I did."

"It's okay, Loc," her mom said. "We're just trying to piece this together."

"So, you're saying it made me sick? That's why I'm here?"

"Not exactly. How many of the pills did you take?"

Lochlan looked at everyone in the room. She chuckled. "Um, just one." When no one else laughed with her, she said, "I just took one—" She again looked at everyone. "Right?"

"You were talking to Spencer on the phone," Vanessa said. "She said that you seemed very groggy and asked her if you had taken your pill. She said that you took one then, so if you had taken one earlier, that makes two."

"So, I took two? And was drinking? God, what an idiot." Lochlan shook her head.

"We think, from the bloodwork, and what we can tell of the missing pills that you had filled three days ago, you had to have taken at least four," the doctor said.

"Four!" Lochlan quickly looked at the doctor, then raised one hand to her forehead at the sudden pain. "I didn't take four!"

"We think that maybe you were drunk, and you kept forgetting you took it," Kayla said.

"I wouldn't have taken four!" Lochlan became agitated. "I didn't. Wouldn't I have been sleepy?"

"Jamie said that sometimes the pills worked, and sometimes they didn't," Kayla reminded her.

"So, I kept thinking I hadn't taken them because they weren't working?"

"We aren't sure exactly what happened," the doctor said. "All we know is that you were drinking heavily, and you were found by a friend unconscious at your residence the next morning."

"Who—"

"Spencer found you," Vanessa said.

"Oh my God." Lochlan put her face in her hands. "She must have been terrified."

"She's pretty shaken up," Vanessa answered. "She's just worried about you."

"So, she brought me here?"

"No, the EMTs did," Lochlan's mom said.

"How sick was I?" Lochlan was in a complete panic now. "If the EMTs were there—" Lochlan's eyes welled up with tears. This was all just too much. "Do people know?" She tried to keep her emotions in check, but then answered her own question. "Of course they know."

"I will leave you ladies alone," the doctor said. "I think the questions that I've asked have cleared things up in my mind."

"Thank you, Doctor," Kayla said.

"Lochlan, your condition could have had a much graver outcome had your friend not found you. When the EMTs arrived, you were starting to aspirate, and that alone…" The doctor paused, watching as the realization dawned on Lochlan as to what could have happened. "It's going to be my recommendation that you aren't prescribed any more medications that can have this effect."

Lochlan only nodded and the doctor left the room. "It's all over the news, isn't it?" When no one answered her, she turned her attention to Vanessa. "I haven't spoken to you in months. How did you find out?"

"Loc—"

"Just tell me." Lochlan felt her lip quiver and that made her even more angry with herself.

Vanessa took a deep breath. "The news."

"And what were they saying?"

"That you were found unresponsive in your home."

"Stop being vague, Vanessa. What did they say!" Lochlan noticed Vanessa's flinch.

"Lochlan—" her mother said.

"I'm sorry." She looked at Vanessa with sincerity. "If you're here, without Jamie hovering over me like a Secret Service agent, it must have been bad. I just want to know—I need to know."

"They said you were found unresponsive with bottles of alcohol and sleeping pills," Vanessa said. "We know that part isn't true. They only found one of each with you."

"Suicide?" Lochlan shook her head. "They think it was a suicide attempt."

"Yes," Vanessa answered.

"Do you think that?" Lochlan looked at Vanessa. "I haven't spoken to you in months and you're standing here. Do you think I tried to kill myself?"

"Spencer talked to you, Loc. She said that you were confused. That's all I have to go on, but no, I think you made a mistake with the pills."

"What does this mean now?"

"The record label may require a treatment facility," her mother answered.

"A what? It was an accident."

"They're saying they have to treat it as if there's a problem because no one actually knows what happened."

"How long?" Her gaze returned to Vanessa.

"As of now, they're saying thirty days inpatient."

"But I didn't mean to!"

"I understand that, and it may be something you can talk to them about, but for now, once you're released, you'll be flown to LA and enter the program."

"What if I refuse?"

"That isn't an option, Loc."

"They are covering their own asses."

"I'd like to think that they're thinking of you as well," her mother said.

"Can I talk to Vanessa alone for a minute?" Lochlan said. She waited a moment after they had left. "What do you think?"

"About what?"

"We haven't spoken in months—"

"Yeah, I know. That's pretty much all you have said since you opened your eyes."

"I just—"

"If it's bothering you that I'm here, I can leave."

"I don't want you to leave. Please don't leave." Suddenly, there were tears in her eyes. "I'm just saying, you found out and you rushed here? Tell me what you thought. Did you come here because you thought I was so depressed that—"

"No! I came here because you were sick and we didn't—" Vanessa's voice cracked. "God, Lochlan, we didn't know what the outcome was going to be. The news was so vague, and I couldn't get in touch with Jamie. I had no clue as to what was happening. Jamie finally called me from your phone and made sure I was here."

"Jamie did that?"

"She did. I hear that the two of you have been having a rough time lately."

Lochlan looked away from Vanessa. "I—I felt like she was to blame, I guess."

"You can't put this on her, Loc. We had a choice, too."

"Did we? Do you think we really had a choice?"

"I know that you two haven't seen eye to eye lately, but Jamie loves you, Loc. She was trying in her own way to protect you. She sees that was wrong now, but at the time, she was honestly doing what she thought was the right thing."

Lochlan almost laughed. "Wow, Jamie getting you here, you defending Jamie…I must have really scared everyone."

"You did."

The sadness of Vanessa's tone stopped Lochlan from teasing any further. "I'm sorry."

"Loc, I get that it was an accident."

"No, I mean I'm sorry. About everything."

"We can talk about all that later. Now probably isn't the time. Right now, we need to work on getting your health issues figured out."

Lochlan took in a deep breath. "I have to do this, Vanessa."

Vanessa looked at her with knowing eyes. "It's my story to tell, and no one gets to take that from me. I don't want to brush this under the rug. I can't sleep without you. I can't eat without you." She looked at Vanessa. "I would go out on that stage every night and perform like a good girl. Then, when the concert was done, the magnitude of what I had lost would hit again. I kept to myself until it was time to turn back into Lochlan Paige. It was like Cinderella. When I stepped on that stage, I was this untouchable star, but when the lights went down, I came back to reality. It didn't make me want to take my life, Vanessa. It only made me want to be better—for you. You deserve someone who can hold your hand and kiss you whenever she wants. I want that for you." She paused. "And I want that to be me."

"Whatever you decide to do, I'm behind you. No matter what happens, I will always be on your side. It's a big decision that affects a lot of people and I understand that, but if you want to go public, I will support you."

"People will be in my business all day, every day. This could involve you too. You have to be ready."

"Lochlan, I am here for you, but this is something you have to do for you. This can't be about us. You have to do this for yourself. Once that is done, we will talk about what that means for us."

"Just don't give up on me yet."

"I won't."

"I am going to kiss you in front of everyone one day."

"I definitely look forward to that if the moment comes." Vanessa smiled at her. "I'm excited for people to see the Lochlan that I know."

"Not with me?"

"Lochlan, nothing has changed."

"I want to be the person you deserve."

"You have to become the person that you deserve first."

Vanessa waited a moment before saying, "I got in."

Lochlan's face lit up. "To Vanderbilt?" Vanessa only nodded. "That's amazing. Congratulations." Lochlan noticed the look of sadness on Vanessa's face. "We'll be in the same town."

"We'll be in the same town," Vanessa repeated.

The smile fell from Lochlan's face as well and she rubbed her face. "It wasn't supposed to be this heavy a moment. We were supposed to be happy about this."

"I can't do this, Lochlan."

"I know."

"I can't be with someone who values their career more than me. That values what that decision could mean for other people more than it could mean for us." Vanessa sighed and took a deep breath. "I can't be last in your world. The last person who you worry may be affected."

"You aren't!"

"It sure as hell feels that way sometimes."

"Just give me a chance to get this right."

Vanessa picked up her things and then turned to Lochlan. "I'm going to get Mia and Ty, and we are heading home. You're okay now, so we need to go—I need to go."

"I'm going to be who you need me to be. I promise."

Vanessa walked over to the bed and wiped at the tear that was running down Lochlan's face. She placed the smallest of kisses to Lochlan's cheek. "I'm glad that you're okay, and I wish only the best for you." With that, Vanessa walked out of her life just as quickly as she had walked in.

CHAPTER SIXTEEN

Ty and Vanessa shared a birthday week each year. Ty's birthday was the beginning of April and Vanessa's was the twenty-fourth. During a weekend between the two, they always did something special. Tonight was no different. They were on their way to a large club outside of Charlotte, where it was open mic night. Ty thought of himself as a Justin Timberlake type; however, he was the only one who thought this. The club held a few hundred people and had a stage. There was a large open floor in front of the stage with tables lining the wall as well as an upstairs balcony full of VIP sections.

They sat in their corner booth as always. Ty and Vanessa knew several of the regulars here and made small talk with them while receiving birthday wishes and shots. As the music started, they cheered on the first performers. A woman did one of Lochlan's songs and Vanessa was instantly sad. She had only talked to Lochlan through texts since leaving the hospital. Mia placed a hand on her knee in comfort. The press had been relentless about Lochlan's accident.

As the song ended, the crowd cheered, and it brought Vanessa back to reality. What she wouldn't give to see Lochlan right now.

❖

Lochlan was snuck in through the back door with the help of the club manager. Once she was tucked away in a supply closet, Jamie stood guard as she warmed up her throat. She smiled as she heard a woman do one of her biggest hits. After several acts had been onstage, Jamie stuck her head inside. "Hey. You okay?"

"Yeah. Did you get the statement out?"

"I did. Lochlan Paige is now officially out as a proud lesbian."

"Remind me not to look at social media." Lochlan laughed.

"I wouldn't. The trending hashtag is 'I stand with Lochlan.' That would completely upset you, I'm sure." They laughed.

"Okay, I'm a little less nervous."

"Don't worry about anything tonight except what you're about to do."

"I love her, Jamie. I have to do this."

"Okay then. She is stage right in a booth against the wall. Let's go get your girl, shall we?"

"I'm right behind you." Lochlan emerged from the room and followed Jamie.

❖

The show director came on the stage and asked, "Are we having a good time?" as the large crowd roared its approval. "Well, that's good, because tonight we have one hell of a surprise for you." The crowd cheered again. "We have a guest performer tonight that you all are gonna *love*! We have had some famous people in the building, but *nothing* like *this* woman." The crowd just kept getting louder. "You ready?"

The director spoke again. "No, I don't think y'all are ready for this." The crowd cheered again, even louder. "All right then. Please welcome...Lochlan Paige." The crowd jumped to their feet and screamed as she walked out onto the stage. The building was literally shaking.

Vanessa heard the "Oh my God" that came from Jenny and Deb. She looked over at her friends' smiling faces as someone joined their table.

Vanessa watched as Spencer squeezed in beside Mia. "What—"

Spencer merely pointed to the stage. "We're looking that way, Ms. Wallace."

Lochlan walked out and was the most nervous that she could ever remember being. She didn't see Vanessa for the sea of standing, screaming women and men. Once they calmed, she walked across the stage and brushed her hand against the fans' outstretched hands. From closer to the edge of the stage, a booth over in the corner came into view and revealed Vanessa, who was still seated. Lochlan was pretty sure it was shock that kept her still. Lochlan couldn't help but smile as she took in the dark-rimmed glasses, blue button-up blouse, and hair that was on point, as curls fell around Vanessa's face and down her shoulders. *There she is.*

Speak, Lochlan, was her next thought. "How are we doing?" The crowd screamed with people yelling "I love you" and "Good." "I heard that it was someone's birthday coming up, so I thought I would just stop in to help her celebrate." The crowd cheered.

Mia looked over at Vanessa. "You need to breathe because if you pass out before I get to see how this shit plays out, I'm gonna be seriously *pissed*." Vanessa's eyes were glassy as she looked over at her. "Breathe, honey. It's really happening."

"I thought I would come out here and sing the birthday

girl a song." Lochlan paused a moment. "Time is a funny thing. I've spent the majority of my adulthood spending every moment doing what I was supposed to, what someone wanted me to, what I thought people expected me to, or what I thought I needed to do to protect the people around me. The last few months I've had a lot of time on my hands. Time to think, to reflect on those things. What it showed me was that I lived a life that was for everyone but me. So, I decided to stop that." The crowd cheered. "So, here I stand, guitar in hand, just trying to impress the girl."

As she strummed the guitar the first time, the crowd quieted. The song was the one she had written the night of the accident. It spoke of love and the power it had to heal the most broken of souls.

Just before the song ended, Lochlan stepped to the edge of the stage and was helped down the stairs. She walked over to Vanessa's table and sang the final words as the music slowed. "The me I am with you is the only me that I need." She slid the guitar down to her side, took Vanessa's face in her hands and said, "If you don't mind, I would like to kiss the girl in front of all these people." Vanessa smiled and nodded her approval and Lochlan kissed her. The crowd erupted into cheers.

Lochlan tried to talk above the screaming. "Do you have any idea how in love with you I am?"

As a tear ran down Vanessa's cheek, she said. "I love you too."

"I promise you will never have to hide again."

Vanessa kissed her again. The deafening screams from their table and the crowd around them faded away, along with all the flashing cameras.

CHAPTER SEVENTEEN

As Lochlan stood in the shower of her hotel room, she thought about the night. She and Vanessa had a quiet dinner while they had talked about everything that had gone on. Vanessa now had three weeks before graduation, and she and Lochlan talked about Lochlan's schedule and how they could work around it. Lochlan had decided to take this tour season off and spend the time with Vanessa. She had lost fans and sponsors, but it wasn't surprising to her.

During the time that she had off, Lochlan had agreed to do something new. While with Mac, she had met one of her friends, Marcus, who was a playwright. He had approached her with an offer to star in a play that was coming to Broadway. It would only be for the summer but would fall during the time Vanessa would have the summer off as well. Vanessa was so excited to see Lochlan on Broadway. It was something she had never thought about but was willing to try.

As rumors started to swirl that Lochlan was taking her shot at Broadway, offers started to come in for guest roles on some of the top-rated television shows. She was even offered a guest role on Mac's show, *Blue Line*. Lochlan couldn't believe that she was ever worried about her career. The name Lochlan Paige was on fire.

"You okay?"

Lochlan opened her eyes to see Vanessa standing outside the glass shower.

Lochlan smiled. "I'm just thinking about everything."

"Need some company?"

"In my thoughts, or the shower?"

Vanessa dropped her robe and opened the door. "Hmm, maybe both?"

Lochlan didn't have time to answer before Vanessa was in the shower and kissing her. Vanessa placed her hand flat against the wall of the oversized shower and Lochlan kissed her way down her body. Her head was thrown back as the water cascaded over her and Lochlan was settled between her legs. The things this woman did to her were unlike anything she had ever experienced. Lochlan seemed to worship every part of her body.

Lochlan felt Vanessa's legs shaking. She softly laughed and spoke. "You need to sit down before you fall."

"Who are you telling?" Vanessa moaned.

Lochlan stood and took Vanessa's hand. "Come on." She stepped out of the shower and Vanessa followed her. As they got to the bed, Vanessa was suddenly over her. "I thought your legs were weak."

"Don't you worry about my legs." Vanessa smiled into the kiss as she pulled her center toward Lochlan's. They rocked together until Lochlan was ready to explode. Lochlan's breathing changed. "Don't you dare just yet."

"I can't do this much longer."

Vanessa ran her hand between them and quickly took Lochlan. Within moments, they both moaned into a kiss. Once Lochlan's breathing evened, she started to laugh. "What the fuck do you do to me?"

"I told you earlier that I would deal with you later."

"You have kept to your word."

Lochlan looked over to the nightstand to see the clock that read 11:15 p.m. "It's almost midnight."

"Got somewhere to be?"

"Nope." Lochlan slid out of the bed.

"Says the woman who is exiting the bed."

"Hang on a second," Lochlan said as she ran out of the bedroom. When she came back into the room, still void of any clothes, she sat on the bed. "Sit up."

"Why?"

"Sit up." She looked down at Vanessa who hadn't moved. "I haven't given you your birthday present yet."

Vanessa sat up. "You're here. You didn't have to give me anything—" She stopped as she saw what Lochlan was holding. It was a small velvet box. "Loc—"

"I remember that night I met you. I thought, 'Here is this smart girl who is making sure that everyone follows the library rules.' You stood over me in those dark-rimmed glasses and that stern look that was trying not to turn into a smile. You shielded me that night and have always tried to do what you thought was in my best interest. I'm pretty sure that I could have told you that I loved you that night you were at the benefit for the Smokeys." She smiled. "I don't think there has ever been a moment that I didn't love you." She took a deep breath. "I'm a lot to deal with. I come with one hundred million Twitter and Instagram followers. I have an army of employees who demand my attention at times, and my schedule can be insane. Not to mention that you may be the focal point of a song, or possibly an entire album." Vanessa laughed. "I love you more than anything and I want to spend the rest of my life hearing that laugh. I am a lot, but I want you. I'll take your feelings regarding any of that into consideration and try to do what is best for the two of us. Just like in the pool, I want to be in all of this life with you." She opened the box to an amazing five-carat cushion cut ring.

"Here's the thing, Vanessa. For a year, I woke up every day thinking that today was the day. Today was the day that you were going to look at me and say that you had been through enough, that you had waited long enough. I chose my career over you from the beginning. Time and time again. All the while, you stood by me. I was so scared of losing what was important to me, what I had worked so hard for, that I lost the only thing that ever truly mattered. I love you and want to marry you. So, Vanessa Wallace, will you do me the honor of joining my insane life and marry me?"

Vanessa was stunned, only nodding her head vigorously. "Yes. Yes!" She kissed Lochlan. It was soft and spoke volumes as to what she felt for her. She could feel the tears that were running down Lochlan's face as they touched her own.

"Did anyone know?" Vanessa asked.

"Just a couple of people." Lochlan counted them off on her fingers. "Your family, my family, your friends, Jamie and Spencer—"

Vanessa laughed. "I will kill them."

"Nessa, honey, it was a surprise."

"Well, congratulations, I'm surprised." Vanessa smiled.

"Also, your parents are patiently waiting on grandkids. Do you know this about them?"

Vanessa laughed and kissed her softly. "I love you, Lochlan."

"I love you too." Lochlan squealed. "We're talking about marriage and kids right now."

"Oh my God, we need people to be screaming with us." She jumped up and grabbed her phone, calling Mia.

Moments later, Mia and Spencer started screaming when they heard the news. Ty screamed just as loud when they called him. It was nearly midnight when the parents were called, and everyone cried. Jamie was called next, and she and Eli offered wholehearted congratulations. It was a wonderful day that had become a monumental night.

During the night, the official Lochlan Paige Twitter and Instagram pages would show a picture of a hand wearing the ring, and a caption that said, "She said yes."

EPILOGUE

One year later...

"Don't be nervous."

"I'm not nervous."

Vanessa looked squarely at her wife. "You are, and it's okay. An EGOT is a big deal."

After Lochlan had finished on Broadway last summer, to amazing reviews, she had added a Tony Award to her shelf. Once it wrapped, she had done a guest spot on one of the longest-running series on television, where she picked up an Emmy. Tonight, was the Oscars, where the rare grouping of awards could be completed. The nomination for Best Original Song had come from a song that she had written for a documentary that was filmed about her journey to come out. It had played in movie theaters around the country and had documented footage of Lochlan's time on the road leading up to the accident that nearly cost the star her life. The documentary was also nominated for Best Documentary Feature. For the past year, the name Lochlan Paige had been gold.

"It is a big deal," Lochlan responded, "but we aren't getting our hopes up."

Vanessa looked at her watch. "Okay, we gotta head that way. Mac is supposed to meet us there."

Vanessa and Mac had become good friends. Mac had been one of the bridesmaids at their wedding, and during the bachelorette party, it had been Mac who Vanessa had stood on a bar and danced with. Mac's best friend, who had attended the wedding with her, had laughed at the display on the bar, and said to Lochlan, "Those two are all yours."

"Yay, me!" Lochlan had laughed as she joined in watching them dance.

During the reception, it had been Mia and Mac who had given the toasts. Vanessa teased Lochlan about nerves now—the wedding was where she saw Lochlan's nerves for the first time. The wedding was filmed during the documentary and they had laughed about Lochlan saying, "What if I cry! Like ugly cry! Like, makeup running down my face, ugly cry? Oh, sweet Jesus, what if I throw up? I may throw up." Lochlan fanned herself. "I feel like I could throw up."

She was brought out of the memory by Vanessa kissing her softly. Lochlan took her in her arms. "If I win, I win. If not, okay. I've gotten the only thing that I've ever needed in life."

Vanessa placed a soft kiss on her lips again. "Good answer. I think you're full of shit, but it was a lovely answer." Lochlan chuckled as Vanessa swatted her ass as she passed her. "Come on, babe, let's go get your EGOT."

Two hours later, they sat in their seats near the documentary crew. They had walked their third red carpet together, and the camera seemed to love Vanessa as much as it did Lochlan. People were starting to shout out Vanessa's name more during the walk. She had her own group of followers and young girls. As a woman who continued her path in school and her career after marrying a very wealthy star, Lochlan was proud of her becoming someone that people could look up to.

Lochlan watched as Mac and her *Blue Line* costar walked to the center of the stage. They made a few jokes, and Mac sobered. "Now, here are your nominees for Best Documentary Feature." They played a clip from each of the films. When it came to Lochlan's film, *Love's Falling Star: The Lochlan Paige Story*, they had shown one of the most powerful moments in the film. The moment that Lochlan awaited a decision from one of the biggest institutions in country music on her status after coming out. The fear that she felt was evident on the screen, but her pride in the life that she now lived was just as apparent. She had been willing to give up that spot for what was right. They showed the clip where Lochlan had talked tearfully about being a fighter. A fighter for women. A fighter for the LGBTQ community. A fighter for equality in life as a member of the human race.

Once the clip was done, the room filled with applause, followed by Mac's voice. "And the winner is..." Mac stopped a moment. Her chin slightly quivered as she said, "The newest member of the EGOT club, Mrs. Lochlan Paige."

Mac jumped with excitement and Lochlan took Vanessa in her arms.

"You did it," Vanessa said into her ear. "I am so proud of you."

"I couldn't have done this without you," Lochlan replied and kissed Vanessa on the cheek as she stood.

She walked to the stage as she wiped a tear from her cheek. Mac met her before she even got to the microphone. They hugged for a moment as Mac congratulated her. Lochlan took the statue from her and looked out over the standing ovation.

Lochlan looked out over the crowd. "As you all know, I've been in the news a lot lately," Lochlan started, and the crowd laughed. "After years of hiding who I was, I decided that it was time to be me." Again, the crowd applauded. "I didn't do anything that I deserve a pat on the back for or something that I should be admired for. I did what I did for one reason—one very selfish reason. I fell in love with someone I refused to do without because of what I do for a living." The crowd applauded again. "I have spent my career looking at people who have come out and said, 'I am so proud of them' or 'They are what makes our community more acceptable.' It was never about *me* coming out. Then when you fall in love with someone, you change. When you love someone, you want to be the best person you can for them. I wanted to be that for someone. I want to be that person that people can look at and say 'If Lochlan Paige can do it, so can I.' I want people to look at me and say, 'I am proud of her,' but more than anything I want the woman that I love to look at me and be proud. My career or my money hasn't impressed her." The crowd laughed. "My being brave enough to be me makes her look at me with not just love, but pride. Every person in this room has that potential to be the person that someone looks at and says, 'If they can, I can.' It's our responsibility, each and every one of us, not just celebrities, but every person, to say 'This is me. This is who I am.' It's up to writers to write parts that not only represent us but represent us *well*. For actors to take roles that depict their, *our,* lives. It's up to LGBTQ network and studio heads to demand those writers and actors get equal chances to tell our story. For the everyday amazing person to help us take on this fight. A fight for the future of the young kid walking the halls of a high school thinking that today is the day they will end their life because they're different. It's time that we all stop allowing people to think we are in such small numbers. We aren't. We have merely allowed them to think that as we hide in our closets and pretend, even to ourselves, that we are invisible. We are not invisible. We are real." The crowd stood in applause. "We are artists. We are actors. We are sports figures. WE. ARE. AMAZING. We deserve love. We are here, and we aren't going away. And we WILL stand for the kids who don't have a voice. We will stand for the ones who are taken to camps, and treated like animals, in the hope that they will change. We must stand together. We must make a better world to leave for these children. I can live with being the person that some look at with disdain in their eyes, because that means someone else is looking at me with hope in theirs. To that teenager in school: You are perfect the way you are. You are wanted, and you are loved. You are valuable, and you are irreplaceable. We, the world, need you just the way you are. You are the one who someday will be someone else's strength. Stay with us and help us fight. We need you for who you are." The crowd's cheering was shaking the cameras at this point. "Thank you for this award." Lochlan saw Vanessa wipe a tear off her cheek. "Vanessa, I love you more than I ever thought imaginable. Thank you for giving me the reason and strength to be the person that I always wanted to be. You are *my* invisible fighter. Thank you." To the sounds of deafening applause from her peers, Lochlan Paige walked off that stage a new, improved, and passionate fighter. She would continue to work for equality and be a voice for the unheard even when, three years later, she would take on her most treasured role: mom.

About the Author

A longtime writer of fan fiction, B.D. Grayson decided that it was time to start writing for more than just fun. She wanted to tell her own stories with characters she had created. Diagnosed with dyslexia as a young child, B.D. found reading more of a chore than a hobby. But she has always been an avid audiobook listener, and she has written fiction since she was a teenager. B.D. developed tools to help with her learning disability, but she still enjoys the ease of listening to a good book.

She married her longtime partner in August 2016. They call Tennessee home.

Books Available From Bold Strokes Books

Fleur d'Lies by MJ Williamz. For rookie cop DJ Sander, being true to what you believe is the only way to live...and one way to die. (978-1-63555-854-8)

Guarding Evelyn by Erin Zak. Can TV actress Evelyn Glass prove her love for Alden Ryan means more to her than fame before it's too late? (978-1-63555-841-8)

Love's Falling Star by B.D. Grayson. For country music megastar Lochlan Paige, can love conquer her fear of losing the one thing she's worked so hard to protect? (978-1-63555-873-9)

Love's Truth by C.A. Popovich. Can Lynette and Barb make love work when unhealed wounds of betrayed trust and a secret could change everything? (978-1-63555-755-8)

Next Exit Home by Dena Blake. Home may be where the heart is, but for Harper Sims and Addison Foster, is the journey back worth the pain? (978-1-63555-727-5)

Not Broken by Lyn Hemphill. Falling in love is hard enough—even more so for Rose, who's carrying her ex's baby. (978-1-63555-869-2)

The Noble and the Nightingale by Barbara Ann Wright. Two women on opposite sides of empires at war risk all for a chance at love. (978-1-63555-812-8)

What a Tangled Web by Melissa Brayden. Clementine Monroe has the chance to buy the café she's managed for years, but Madison LeGrange swoops in and buys it first. Now Clementine is forced to work for the enemy and ignore her former crush. (978-1-63555-749-7)

A Far Better Thing by JD Wilburn. When needs of her family and wants of her heart clash, Cass Halliburton is faced with the ultimate sacrifice. (978-1-63555-834-0)

Body Language by Renee Roman. When Mika offers to provide Jen erotic tutoring, will sex drive them into a deeper relationship or tear them apart? (978-1-63555-800-5)

Carrie and Hope by Joy Argento. For Carrie and Hope, loss brings them together but secrets and fear may tear them apart. (978-1-63555-827-2)

Detour to Love by Amanda Radley. Celia Scott and Lily Andersen are seatmates on a flight to Tokyo and by turns annoy and fascinate each other. But they're about to realize there's more than one path to love. (978-1-63555-958-3)

Ice Queen by Gun Brooke. School counselor Aislin Kennedy wants to help standoffish CEO Susanna Durr and her troubled teenage daughter become closer—even if it means risking her own heart in the process. (978-1-63555-721-3)

Masquerade by Anne Shade. In 1925 Harlem, New York, a notorious gangster sets her sights on seducing Celine, and new lovers Dinah and Celine are forced to risk their hearts, and lives, for love. (978-1-63555-831-9)

Royal Family by Jenny Frame. Loss has defined both Clay's and Katya's lives, but guarding their hearts may prove to be the biggest heartbreak of all. (978-1-63555-745-9)

Share the Moon by Toni Logan. Three best friends, an inherited vineyard, and a resident ghost come together for fun, romance, and a touch of magic. (978-1-63555-844-9)

Spirit of the Law by Carsen Taite. Attorney Owen Lassiter will do almost anything to put a murderer behind bars, but can she get past her reluctance to rely on unconventional help from the alluring Summer Byrne and keep from falling in love in the process? (978-1-63555-766-4)

The Devil Incarnate by Ali Vali. Cain Casey has so much to live for, but enemies who lurk in the shadows threaten to unravel it all. (978-1-63555-534-9)

Secret Agent by Michelle Larkin. CIA Agent Peyton North embarks on a global chase to apprehend rogue agent Zoey Blackwood, but her commitment to the mission is tested as the sparks between them ignite and their sizzling attraction approaches a point of no return. (978-1-63555-753-4)

LOVE'S
FALLING STAR